Warning: Wicked Web
The Sinister Society

Crimson Cult Media

Chapter 1
Broccoli-Head

L.W. Young

Leon was still half asleep when he checked his phone in the dark. He saw Dylan's WhatsApp message:

'Help me'

Leon wiped his eyes tiredly.

"Christ," Leon moaned, swinging his feet out of bed, "what has that dumb kid gotten himself into now?"

Sitting in the dark, Leon replied with a single question mark. He waited, but there was no answer. Leon crashed back against the mattress and stared blankly at the ceiling. It was late, he was tired, and he wanted nothing more than to ignore Dylan's message and get back to sleep, but he found himself up on his feet and picking clothes out of the wardrobe instead. Apparently, old habits refused to die.

"I hope that kid appreciates everything I do for him," Leon thought as he threw on a navy blue hoodie and joggers and did a few stretches to wake himself up, "not that he'd understand anything about 'appreciation'."

He found himself wondering how he had gotten stuck with this: the only bodyguard gig an ex-military, Terry Crews-looking dude like him could apparently land; protecting some snotty rich kid who liked to play cruel pranks on random members of the public. There must be a better way to pay for his retirement than this.

"There was a better way... once," Leon thought bitterly, grabbing his water bottle from the fridge and taking a sip, "but it's over now."

He felt another buzz in his pocket.

Letting the fridge door hang open, Leon fished his phone out with one hand and checked Dylan's reply.

'*Turn on my stream,*' it simply said.

Leon sighed and rolled his eyes up to the ceiling.

"Weird..." he grumbled, thumbing through the phone to bring up the Kick Stream app Dylan had made him download, "but whatever..."

The feed took a few seconds to load, but what Leon saw made him immediately drop his water bottle. A cold sweat broke out all over his body and his hand crept up to his mouth.

"Jesus..." he uttered, "what the fuck is this?"

The stream showed Dylan tied to a chair with blood trickling down his face. He was uncharacteristically quiet, but that was because there was tape over his mouth. The room around him was dark, but dim lights had been set up just carefully enough to show glimpses of Dylan's living room while obscuring the shape standing behind him. This figure had its hands grasping Dylan's neck, and its fingers were a bright, sickly green.

"No..." Leon trembled, almost dropping his phone, "it... it can't be..."

The looming figure was a tall, gangly shape with sickly green skin and a dark shadow covering his face. The figure wrapped its slender fingers around Dylan's skinny throat, its dirty nails tickling the fluff of Dylan's facial hair.

"I can't wait..." this mysterious figure giggled gleefully, stroking Dylan's bushy head as its voice crackled through the phone speakers, "... I can't wait, to... to chop. Him. UP!"

After this, Leon swiftly pocketed his phone, grabbed the 9mm pistol from his closet, and raced down the apartment stairs to his car.

"Please let this not be what I think it is," Leon's thoughts pounded as he sprinted down the spiralling stairwell, "Please let this not be about what happened earlier…"

Even Leon thought that Dylan had taken this morning's prank too far.

They'd been in a Walmart, somewhere Dylan would never have gone unless it was to mess with people, and Dylan had been jumping up and down excitedly while his equally vapid friend and sometimes cameraman, Ritchie, trailed along behind him like a faithful puppy. Leon, meanwhile, followed with his hands in his pockets, mentally checked out.

The pair had been loudly yapping on about Fortnite and OnlyFans models or some shit, until Dylan suddenly went quiet, and a lightbulb seemed to go off in his head (a rare occurrence).

"Hey, I've just thought of a cool idea for a video!" Dylan suddenly declared, making a dash for the nearest customer. "Make sure you're streaming this, Ritchie!"

Dylan and Ritchie tittered to each other and raced on ahead, zoning in on a tall, spectacled man with teenage acne and a bald spot of someone in their late 40s. Dylan and Ritchie bounded up to the slump-shouldered man like cackling hyenas, circling him.

"Hey man, how's it going?" Dylan bellowed in the lanky man's face while he had been innocently browsing the aisle. "Say hi to the folks in chat!"

Their startled victim remained oblivious as Dylan held up his phone to take a selfie with the hapless guy. Leon hung back at a safe distance, obliged to step in if something happened. He made a mental note to pick up a dirt-cheap bottle of bourbon on his way out, as he'd probably need it after this was over.

"What..." the 40-year-old dweeb said. "What do you youngsters want?"

"We're just chillin', my man," Dylan now leered into the shopper's face while Ritchie still aimed the camera at them. "After all, we know all about what you've been up to!"

At this, the shopper's back went up, and he pushed his glasses up his nose. Leon wondered if it was this guy's way of trying to look tough.

"Listen." The shopper collected himself, making himself taller. "I don't know what you think you're doing here, but..."

Dylan, not listening, quickly interrupted him.

"So, how come you're here trying to meet 14-year-old girls?" Dylan retorted gleefully with a mean grin on his face. "Huh?"

The only people who seemed to find this funny were Dylan and Ritchie. Meanwhile, the prank victim, Leon, and everyone else in the store within earshot went quiet. After getting over his shock, the shopper tried to say something, but Dylan wasn't even remotely interested in hearing it.

"Hey everybody, listen up. This creep is here to meet a 14-year-old!" Dylan cupped his mouth and hollered into the store. "We have chat logs and everything to prove it!"

"N... now listen here!" The shopper's mustache twitched as he lowered his voice into a growl. "I don't know who you think you are, but that's not the kind of thing you go around saying about people!"

Leon groaned inwardly. From his indignant manner and prideful tone, he now understood that this random shopper was once probably teased by spoiled rich preps like Dylan himself back in high school and was now an embittered old Charles Bronson wannabe. These kinds of righteous fucks were *always* trouble. Whipping his hands out of his pockets, Leon stepped towards the action with his palms raised defensively.

"Ooooh, what are you going to do?" Dylan raised his arms and wiggled his fingers dramatically at his prank victim. "You gonna get me?"

"No." The shopper peered down his nose at Dylan, with menace in his voice, "But Broccoli Head will."

Not understanding what the heck this strange man was talking about, Dylan flipped the guy off and turned away. Ritchie, still chortling, had caught the act and reaction on camera, so the fun was over. However, the balding man certainly wasn't done. He grabbed Dylan by the scruff of his white sports shirt and pulled him back.

"You hear me!?" the shopper hissed, catching flecks of spit in his mustache as he pulled Dylan towards him. "Broccoli Head will chop. You. UP!"

"H... hey, GET OFF ME!" Dylan reeled, his glee instantly turning to panic as he reached out for help. "LEON, HEEEELLLPP!"

Perhaps a little too forcefully, Leon had ripped the shopper's hand off Dylan's collar and shoved him back against the shelves, making a few cans fall onto the floor, and stepping between the pair. Ritchie, meanwhile, just stood gormlessly and watched, apparently incapable of sentient thought when faced with a situation that involved more than just pointing a camera and laughing.

"My designer shirt!" Dylan cried miserably while inspecting the damage the shopper's nails had done to his collar, then looking back at him hatefully with tears stirring in his eyes. "This shirt cost more money than you make in a year, you FUCKING PIECE OF SHIT!"

Meanwhile, the spectacled man kept trying to lock eyes with Dylan, peering over Leon's shoulder.

"Look, man, I don't want to hurt you," Leon hushed, trying to get the man's attention, "but I'm gonna need you to chill, alright?"

But the man refused to take his attention off Dylan, delighting in the boy's misery at the damage done to his precious little designer shirt.

"Oh, that won't be anything compared to what Broccoli Head will do when he finds you; do you hear me?" The man smiled, repositioning his glasses again. "He's gonna sniff you out, track you down, and he's gonna KILL you. ALL OF YOU!"

Then, with mad laughter, the man jabbed his finger at Ritche's camera while making sure he was in center frame.

"In fact," the man said, smiling, "he's probably watching all this right NOW!"

Broccoli Head. Leon was familiar with it as a term for a particular kind of Gen-Z haircut, popular with influencers and the Tik-Tok crowd, and one that Dylan himself proudly sported. Curly head on top, shaved at the sides. Broccoli. Any modern barber would know what the term meant. But this guy clearly wasn't referring to any kind of haircut. He was referring to a person. A *thing*.

"What are you talking about, man?" Leon hushed again, mentally blocking out Dylan's pleas for violence against the offender.

Turning his eyes on Leon, the man's grin became even wider. His cracked lips peeled up his dirty teeth and made Leon wince at his rotten-beef-tasting breath.

"You've never heard of him, son?" the man whispered giddily. "He's out there, always on the prowl for bad little boys and girls who use the internet to hurt people, and then he GETS THEM!"

"What the hell are you talking about, FREAK!?" Dylan now cried tearfully, battering Leon's massive shoulders with his tiny fists to try and prompt him into action, "Leon, kick this guy's ass already!"

"What's the problem here?"

The whole party turned and saw two members of store security, as well as the store manager, close in on the group with their arms folded across their chests. Leon stepped away from the prank victim with his arms up, but Dylan stepped forward and pointed a stubby finger right in his face.

"This guy attacked me!" Dylan hissed, wiping away tears. "Arrest him, not us!"

The two security clerks looked at each other and shared a smirk, and then turned to Leon with a lowly, disapproving look. Leon looked at the ground, ashamed.

"Is this true?" The store manager tried to get Leon's attention.

Leon raised his head to say something, but Dylan cut in over him.

"Oh, and he's also been talking to minors online!" Dylan suddenly remembered, squaring back up to the prank victim. "We have the chat logs to prove everything. Arrest him now!"

At Dylan's words, Leon backed down. With hard eyes, the manager turned her head to the cowering, bespectacled man to try to get his take on things. However, she then saw Ritchie's camera.

"Is..." she hesitated, pointing at the phone's lens, "is this live?"

Ritchie nodded, and the manager seemed to falter, no longer interested in talking to the victim. Leon recognised the expression in her eyes. He'd seen it so many times while working for Dylan. She didn't want to get caught making a mistake on camera.

"How many viewers?" the security guard asked.

"Thousands!" Dylan smirked, locking eyes with the victim and daring him to fight back. "If not more!"

The two security guards looked at each other hesitantly, while the store manager gulped dryly. Leon couldn't help but die a little inside, was that all it took these days to convict someone of a crime, for some popular rich kid on the internet to say you did it?

'Well, if it is,' Leon thought shamefully, 'then I guess I'm part of the problem.'

"We... we'll detain the old guy on your word," the manager then decided, motioning for the two security guards to haul him away. "Now, the rest of you, get out of here!"

Leon started to say something but backed down as Dylan gave him a chastising look. Meanwhile, the two security guards swooped in on either side of the glasses-wearing prank victim and grabbed his arms. He looked at them, startled.

"Come on, pal," the first security guard said, pulling him along. "Let's go have a private chat, huh?"

The old guy started to resist, but then spotted Dylan. The kid was clearly in a fluster: his face was beet red, he was panting hard, and tears were still stirring in his eyes. Sensing something of a victory, the man actually smiled as he let the guards lock his arms and push him away for questioning.

"Broccoli Head, boys," the old guy hollered back at them as he was dragged away. "He'll find you... tonight!"

"Stupid, stupid, STUPID!" Leon raged, slamming his fist against the steering wheel, "I kept telling him something like this would happen one day, but he wouldn't listen!"

Leon had even tried to tell the kid something similar right after the event had happened while they'd been fleeing the scene of the crime. However, Dylan had seemed more preoccupied with what his chat group was saying about it on his phone screen.

Now, waiting at a set of traffic lights on the dark highway, Leon was caught between keeping his eyes on the road and his *own* phone, checking that the troublesome kid's antics hadn't gotten him killed. Dylan was still breathing, but the knife in the hands of the hidden, green-fingered kidnapper was now carving a line across the top of Dylan's forehead, spilling a curtain of blood across his face. The boy screamed through his tape gag.

Leon almost threw up.

'Keep it together, Leon,' he demanded of himself. 'Remember, you saw way worse stuff than this in Afghanistan.'

But that was just it, wasn't it? In the military, he'd been trained not to cry, trained not to run away, trained not to lose his mind at the sight of an innocent child being a casualty of war. He was trained to reject his humanity and fight it down. The only problem was, he'd told himself that all these things would be different once he got home. None of his military training had prepared him for the shock of coming home to find his house empty, his fiancée gone, and his baby boy taken along with her. After all the horrors he'd seen on the battlefield, was he now going to start crying because his old life was gone? Of course he was! No training had prepared him for that.

"So, why can't I do the same now?" he asked himself while his glassy eyes waited for the light to go green, "Dylan doesn't respect me either, so why can't I just walk away?"

But Leon knew that the answer was right in front of him; it was because Leon didn't have anyone else now. Not all hope was lost. Dylan was just a kid; there was still time for him to learn about respecting others, and with terminally absent parents and dumbass friends like Ritchie, was it even any wonder Dylan had turned out to be such a brat? Lord knew, Lord KNEW, that Leon had tried his darndest to set Dylan straight whenever he could. Even if he didn't listen, Dylan might just be the closest thing to a son Leon had left...

Suddenly, a screaming horn blared behind him as light filled the cabin. On instinct, Leon's arm reached up for the 9mm under his shirt as a passing car went tearing past. Shellshocked, Leon gripped his fists around the wheel until they went pale. The light ahead had been green for some time.

Breathing hard, Leon realized that he needed to do something with all this stress, anger and pain. Maybe he should forget about Dylan, chase that driver down, and pump him full of lead. Wouldn't that be satisfying? But Leon was pulled away from his anger when something on the phone screen caught his attention. Forcing himself to look, Dylan saw that Broccoli Head, or whoever this knife-wielding maniac was, had finished carving a line across Dylan's forehead and was now dragging the blade down towards Dylan's ear, drawing a red outline of Dylan's hairline.

"Is he..." Leon muttered to himself, drawing a sharp intake of breath, "Is he *scalping* him?"

But this wasn't the only thing that sent a shiver of shock into the pit of Leon's stomach and made his blood boil. Also on the screen was Dylan's live chat window, which crawled up the screen with what Dylan's followers were saying about him. And they were *laughing* at him.

'Dylan is so cooked!' said one reply that received tens of laugh reacts within the second it was uploaded. This was one of the nicer comments. Meanwhile, the viewer count hovered at the 1K mark, and yet nobody was doing a damned thing about it. Was it any wonder that Dylan had turned out the way he did when surrounded with fans like this? What did the kids call it these days, 'hate watching'? Did they *honestly* just want to see him suffer?

Leon suddenly realised what he had to do.

"Hang on, son," Leon muttered, wiping sweat off his face. "Hang on, daddy's coming..."

Screeching to a halt, Leon's car ripped up the manicured lawn outside Dylan's parent's house. The last thing Leon had heard from the live feed, still broadcasting from his phone, was Dylan's muffled wails as his sick torturer continued the game. Gripping his pistol with both hands, Leon sprinted across the garden in the dark towards Dylan's front door.

This Broccoli Head guy, or whoever it really was, probably knew Leon was here, so there was no need for subtlety anymore. Leon supposed the smart thing to do would have been to call the police, but Dylan was his responsibility. He had to deal with this alone.

Racing up to the front door, Leon readied a lunging kick, which had served him well in Afghanistan when rooting out terrorist hideouts. Leon's boot crashed against the door, but it stood firm, not even budging. Leon recoiled, trying to numb himself to the new pain in his leg.

"Gotta try for the window now," Leon grunted, forcing himself to run, "gotta move!"

Leon arrived at the huge picture window, which would look in on the darkened living room if the blinds weren't shut. Leon heard screaming on the other side.

"Hang on, Dylan!" Leon couldn't help himself, crying out as he raised his firearm to the window and shielded his eyes. "I'm coming!"

But wait, what if he accidentally shot Dylan? Thinking on his feet, Leon turned the aim of his weapon to the left of the window, keeping the muzzle at eye level so the double-glazed windows would still give way, but avoiding the center of the room where Leon remembered Dylan to be sitting in the video.

Leon fired five times.

The reinforced window allowed the final bullet through, creating a lattice of splintering glass that Leon knew he could shatter if he applied all his strength. After taking a short run up across Dylan's now utterly devastated lawn, Leon dived through the window. It broke, and he tumbled into the darkened living room with a crash.

Lying on his side, the cracked glass softening his fall, Leon raised his gun in both hands to where Dylan's captor should have been standing. The lights were angled just as they had been in the video, casting a purple hue on the empty space with bloodstains pooling on the carpet and an overturned chair with strips of duct tape glued to it.

But no one was there.

Rising to his feet, Leon noticed the tripod with the video camera mounted on it, propped up and looking at him with its red recorder light still beaming. Right now, thousands of Dylan's viewers were probably watching him lying here on the floor…

Then Leon heard footsteps creep up behind him. Leon turned around and grabbed the attacker with both hands. As Leon raised his fist, the defenceless figure before him raised its gangly, green hands in protest.

"Stop, STOP dude!" the surprisingly high-pitched squeal came out. "Oh man, don't hurt me, PLEASE!"

Leon let the person go, realising they were just a kid, and allowed them to go reeling up against the wall where they cowered with their arms raised. With rising anger upon seeing the smartphone held in one of his hands, Leon realised that he recognised the boy.

"Ritchie!?" Leon released a deep sigh, lowering his arms. "What the fuck are you *doing* here, man?"

"I... it was all a prank," Ritchie shivered, still refusing to look at the big guy. "We... we were just pranking you... for Dylan's channel."

With his hands held out in the half-light through the shattered window, Leon could see Ritchie's hands covered with green paint and penned-on veins. On video, they'd looked like the hands of a monster, but now he could see it for the fake Halloween make-up it really was.

"Pranking me?" Leon hissed, locking eyes with Ritchie. "But what about the blood?"

Ritchie reached a shaking hand into his shorts and pulled out something that looked like a prop knife with a concealed button that sprayed red corn syrup from its tip. Leon quickly recognised it as the one from the video.

"A... after what that guy said in the store earlier, we thought it would make a good video," Ritchie smirked sheepishly, "... got you, heh."

As his muscles started to relax, Leon felt for the living room light switch and turned it on. Seeing the little rich, white kid cowering underneath him made him instinctively want to help him up, but he just couldn't do it.

"Why?" Leon asked, eyes glazed over with hurt, "I... I've only ever tried to be like a father to Dylan..."

"Hey, I wouldn't take it so personally, man. That's just the way he is." Ritchie laughed nervously, rising to his feet. "The other day, he emptied an entire bottle of cleaning fluid over my head without warning, just so he could film it. We both had a good laugh..."

Yeah, a good laugh. One big joke, just like Leon's entire life had been one big joke. Oh, you cared about someone, Leon? Turns out they didn't ever give a damn about you. You're on your own now, buddy. But hey, at least it made for some good content, right? *Right?*

Then, Leon's sadness and disappointment was quickly replaced by hot rage. His clenched fists started to shake at his sides.

"Where the fuck is that kid?" Leon seethed, punching his hands together. "Forget Broccoli-Head, *I'm* gonna kill him!"

At this, Ritchie looked up like a prairie dog out of a burrow, sniffing the air curiously.

"Good question. He... he was supposed to jump out with me," he said, pointing towards the other end of the room. "We were supposed to surprise you together."

Leon followed Ritchie's finger and peered over the couch to his right. That's where Leon saw Dylan lying slumped down against the wall in the space behind the couch, just out of Leon's view. Dylan was covered in blood (or corn syrup, or ketchup, or whatever the hell it was), but his trademark 'Broccoli' haircut remained completely untouched. Rolling his eyes, Leon went over to him.

"Quit playing dead, idiot," Leon sighed, kicking the kid's limp leg. "You think I'm gonna fall for this again?"

But Dylan didn't move.

Then Leon noticed that there was a bullet hole through Dylan's precious designer shirt at the exact same angle where Leon had fired through the window...

The End

L.W. Young graduated from the University of Kent with a BA Honors degree in English literature and creative writing. He has experience with writing for theater, film and YouTube, and is a passionate advocate of mindfulness and raising awareness of mental health issues. His favourite authors and influences include an eclectic bag: ranging from Stephen King to Cormac McCarthy to Ray chandler to David Mitchell to Kazuyo Ishigoda to Margaret Atwood and Colson Whitehead. However, if you ask him, he would probably tell you his favourite books are the Point Horror novels he read in his High School library as a teenager. His haunting novella, THE OCCUPANT, debuts April 2025.

Chapter 2
Swipe Right For Death
Carietta Dorsch

The room was dark and silent, the only sound being the soft hum of the computer as it sat on the desk in the corner. The girl sat hunched over the screen, her eyes red and swollen from crying. She just wanted a friend, someone to talk to online, but everyone was inactive. They were all probably enjoying their real-life get-togethers and parties. She didn't have any RL friends, only online ones. And right now they were nowhere to be found as she struggled desperately to hold on to her sanity as the wave of depression hit her like a sledgehammer to the head.

Suddenly, her screen opened up to her email account.

"What the fuck?"

The message contained a single link, ominous in its simplicity. Without hesitation, Rachel clicked on it. In an instant, her screen flickered and went dark, only to come back to life with a new interface she had never seen before.

const emailData1 = {

sender: XXX,

content: **'Hi Rachel, welcome to SwipeRight'**

};

const emailData2 = {

sender: 'XXX',

content: **'Rachel, swipe left for those you like, and right for those who will..........'**

};

Her screen flashed and turned into a bunch of head-shots on her screen as if she were playing a virtual game of Guess Who, and then it flashed multiple colors and back to the photos of men and women's headshots.

const emailData3 = {

sender: 'XXX',

content: '**Rachel, swipe left for those you like, and right for those who will..........**'

};

There were several men who were attractive, and some very beautiful women. She didn't know where to start. Her bisexuality was in overdrive, trying to decide which side of the coin needed polishing the most.

She swiped left on a gorgeous blonde woman and the screen flashed to a video of that very woman leaning over a kitchen counter, pleasuring herself with a carrot and licking a watermelon.

"What the fuck?"

The blonde slid the carrot in and out of herself, and the wet popping of her hand smacking into her wet thighs almost drowned out the noise of her sucking lips on the watermelon pieces as she slurped them in her eager mouth.

"What the fuck is this?"

Rachel hit the close-out button to the video. Her screen flashed once, and again the row of headshots popped up onto the screen.

This was some kind of sex video thing. Where you watch as they watch kind of thing. Right?

She looked at each picture slowly as she tried to convince herself this was okay to do.

It has been a while since I had sex, and I haven't had a partner in years.

She swiped left on a cute dark-haired man who looked to be in his early twenties, a young Johnny Depp type of face.

The screen flashed and a video of the very man she picked humping the back of a wicker chair. A hole was made and his hard cock poked in and out as he poured honey on it as he thrust through it

He grunted with each push and eventually, the honey bottle was completely emptied, and he grabbed a jar of grape jelly to pour over his long, rigid semen torpedo just as he began to shoot off rope after rope of white cum through the hole like a bullseye target on a dartboard.

"What the fuck?" she almost yelled to the screen, just like she did when watching the dumb girls in horror movies. "What the actual fuckety is wrong with you, sir?"

She hit the close-out button.

const emailData4 = {

sender: 'XXX',

content: **'Rachel, you have used your two close-out options you are allowed within an hour.**

Next video you will be forced to watch without skipping.'

```
  };
```

"As if. I will close out whenever I want and on whatever I want," she told her computer as if it were a living person.

The computer screen flickered, and several shades of green and blue flipped and flopped on the screen like a pair of dancing jump ropes before the screen flashed to a video of her parents in bed. They were sleeping, but in the corner there stood a man in a black hoodie and a burlap mask holding a rifle to her father's head.

The screen flashed again, and this time, the colors yellow and red danced on the screen like battling strings before the message appeared.

```
const emailData5 = {
  sender: 'XXX',
```

content: 'Rachel, you WILL play by the rules or your family will die.'

};

const emailData6 = {

sender: 'XXX',

content: 'Rachel, swipe left for those you like, and right for those who will..........'

};

Fear gripped Rachel's mind as she realized that someone was watching her, someone who could see her and keep her in this sick game by force. She looked around her room frantically, searching for any signs of an intruder, but there was nothing. She was alone, trapped in a nightmare that seemed all too real.

With trembling fingers, Rachel was about to type on the screen, but instead the screen wavered once more in its lines of colors and flashes, and the same message appeared: "Rachel, swipe left for those you like, and right for those who will..."

The video of her parents appeared once more.

Then the message.

const emailData7 = {

sender: 'XXX',

content: **'PLAY OR THEY DIE!!'**

};

The headshots come up onto her screen once more. She was sweating and fighting for breath. Her panic was kicking in to an extreme degree. Body shaking and mind running a million miles an hour, she swiped right on a young man who favored a young Brad Pitt.

The Brad Pitt lookalike was sitting in a room with a man behind him pointing a pistol at a small little girl. She heard him say something that sounded like, 'Do it or else,' but wasn't sure. The man was shaking and sweating, and let out a groan of misery and dread as he picked up a cheese grater.

The man on the screen began grinding his face with a cheese grater, the sound of metal against flesh echoing through the room and through her computer speakers like a sharp scrape from a chalkboard. Skin and flesh rolled off in bloody ribbons, piling up on the floor like loose thread for a ball of yarn as blood flowed freely from the wounds. His eyes were wide with a mixture of pain and shame, a frown of utter despair spreading across his mutilated face.

Tears welled up in her eyes, a mixture of disgust and pity for the man on the screen. She wanted to look away, to escape the nightmare unfolding before her, but she was frozen in place, unable to tear her eyes away from the screen.

Her screen flashed to her parents' room, then the screen flashed once more.

```
const emailData8 = {

sender: 'XXX',

content: 'WATCH OR THEY DIE!!'

};
```

The room was dimly lit, the only source of light coming from the flickering screen that displayed the gruesome scene once again. The man's hands were covered in blood and chunks of flesh, the cheese grater now stained a deep crimson glistened in the lamplight of his computer. He continued to grind away at his face, the sound growing more wet and sloshy.

As the minutes passed, the man's face became unrecognizable, a mangled mess of torn flesh and exposed muscle. Lines of muscle fell, and flesh flopped and his teeth could be seen all the way around his mouth from the openings in his face. The pain must have been excruciating, but he seemed to push forward, a look of panic and determination on his face. He was no doubt suffering in order to save his daughter.

Finally, the man stopped grinding his face, the cheese grater clattering to the floor. He looked directly at the camera, his eyes glazed over with sadness and the look of defeat. And then, as the man behind him cocked his pistol, the man who no longer looked like Brad Pitt, but a spilled package of raw hamburger, raised a bloody hand to his mouth and began to eat the chunks of flesh that had fallen from his face. His fingers digging into the strips of meat, and pulling the strands off like Band-Aids.

He shoved these strips into his mouth as if he were eating strips of taffy, and chewed with a disgusted look. He gagged as he tried to swallow.

The screen flashed back to the headshots and then the message:

```
const emailData10 = {
```

sender: 'XXX',

content: '**Congratulations, you have passed round three of five. You must watch two more videos to save your family.**'

};

Looking at the faces staring back at her on the screen she realized she was playing with their lives. She tried to remain calm, to think.

Okay, if I swipe left I see their kink. If I swipe right they torture themselves. So, I mean left is the only way to save them. Isn't it? If I pick right they die, so I am going with left.

She chose a tall, handsome man who looked like a bodybuilder or a professional MMA fighter. His muscles were so huge and chiseled.

He looked directly into the camera and smiled as he yanked on his penis as if he were trying to start a lawn mower. He beat it quick and fast, his hand moving so fast that it looked like he was just flapping his hand around, and then suddenly he stopped. Letting his hand fall away from his cock, she saw he was packing at least a foot long, maybe even longer.

Then she heard a noise.

But not just any noise.

It was the sound of a baby crying.

What the fuck!?

The man placed a small bundle of joy in front of him and then...

Rachel recoiled in disgust, bile rising in her throat. The scene was too much to bear. Rachel quickly tried to shut off the screen, but her computer wasn't responding.

const emailData10 = {

sender: 'XXX',

content: '**YOU CHOSE THEIR FATE**'

};

The screen flashed, and her parents were on the screen once again. She jumped up, and ran to her bedroom door, but the door was locked. She frantically tried to open it, but it wouldn't budge. She picked up her lamp and began beating the door as tears fell from her face.

"Please, no! I didn't know what I was clicking on. I didn't understand!"

Then a loud gunshot, followed by another.

She looked at the screen and saw her parents both dead. A pool of blood forming around them on the mattress from their headshot wounds.

"Please! No! No! No!"

const emailData11 = {

sender: 'XXX',

content: '**GAME OVER**'

};

"No! This can't be real! This can't be real!"

Suddenly, she felt a hand around her throat and a cloth over her mouth.

Then, there was darkness.

const emailData11 = {

sender: 'XXX',

content: '**SMILE FOR YOUR HEADSHOT**'

};

Waking up and shaking off the fog of having lost consciousness, she felt like she had been hit with a brick upside her face. She looked up and around the room; the screen caught her attention. It was blinking a bright neon pink and was making a giggling, laughing similar to those pull-string dolls her sister was obsessed with collecting.

const emailData12 = {

sender: 'XXX',

content: '**YOU ARE ON CAMERA. USE WHAT IS IN FRONT OF YOU, OR YOUR SISTER DIES!**'

};

No. No. No. This can't be happening!

A man's voice came from behind her. "Do not turn around."

"What...what...," she was stumbling over her words as fear took hold of her mind.

"Use what is in front of you, or your sister dies."

"Why are you doing this?" her voice watery from tears. "Why are you..."

"Use what is in front of you, or your sister dies."

"But, why are you..." she would have screamed if her voice weren't so hoarse from crying.

"Five, four, three, two,..."

"Okay. Okay."

The man stopped counting as Rachel picked up the egg beater. The blades had been sharpened and the handle's plastic was coated in dried blood, but it could have been rust; she just wasn't sure. It wasn't as if she was truly thinking straight. She was too afraid.

She stared at the egg beater, wondering what he wanted her to do. The man grew audibly annoyed as she took her time to come to the conclusion.

"You want me to..." her voice wavy and shaking.

"Yes. Do it now. Last chance."

Spreading her legs apart, her skirt rose up, exposing her sex to the camera's full view.

Tears continued to well in her eyes.

Her lips shook and her breathing hitched as she looked down at the egg beater.

She slowly pushed the egg beater into her most intimate parts, feeling a sharp white-hot pain shoot through her body like a million push pins hitting every nerve ending. The blades cut into her flesh, causing a wave of blood to gush out of her mangled vaginal walls as she pushed it deeper within herself. She let out a guttural screech as her wrist finally reached her clitoris and the excruciating pain of having the whole piece inside consumed her.

She sat there as blood trickled down her thighs and around the eggbeater's blades, flowing underneath her and soaking the seat cushion. Her chest heaved once, twice; it was hard to breathe as the pain used up her every thought.

"You know what to do," he said.

Tears streamed down her face as she turned the handle of the egg beater, feeling the blades tear through her insides, ripping her walls and destroying her innermost private places. The anguish was unbearable, like a thousand rusty knives stabbing into her at once. Blood shot out in all directions, splattering against the desk, running down her thighs., and a jet stream shot out and hit the computer screen.

She was sitting in a puddle of her own blood, the metallic scent and the salty aroma of her tears filling the air. The room was spinning, her vision blurred by the overpowering pain.

As she continued to twist the handle of the eggbeater, the pain intensified. It felt like her entire body was on fire, burning like a wildfire, every nerve ending shrieking in agony, telling her to stop, but she knew she couldn't. She had to save her sister. She could feel herself slipping away as the loss of blood grew more rapid and steady.

And then, suddenly, the eggbeater fell from her hands, clattering to the floor. She collapsed from the chair, gasping for breath, her legs covered in blood.

But as she lay there, broken and bleeding, the screen

flashed to a message:

const emailData13 = {

sender: 'XXX',

content: '**Congratulations!!! You saved your sis-**

ter,

or did you?

You'll never know.'

};

const emailData14 = {

sender: 'XXX',

content: '**DEAR READER...GO CHECK YOUR**

EMAILS. THERE SHOULD BE SOMETHING

THERE FOR YOU............'

};

Carietta Dorsch has loved horror movies since she was a little girl watching them at a way too earlier age and loves even more to share her love of horror with her writing. She also writes poetry, romance, and true crime. Find more of her work "Oh Come All Ye Fearful," "Never Be Lonely Again," "Scream and Cream," "The Mitchell County Stories," "Cannibalistic Loneliness," and "Tattered."

Chapter 3
Highest Bidder

Andy H

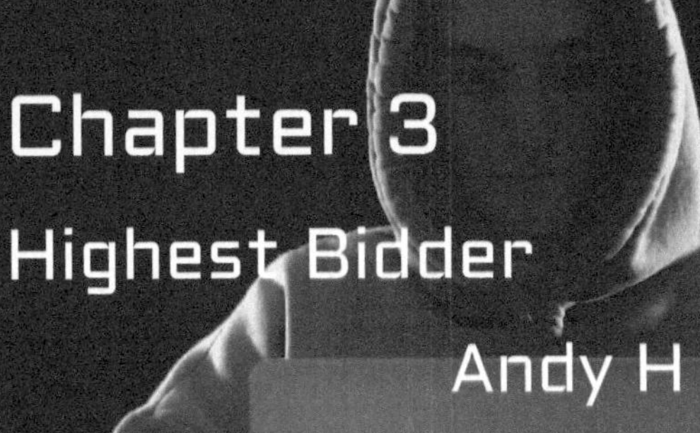

The trolley rolled down the dark, dank hallway, its small wheels slowing its progress every time they hit a rut or a crack in the concrete. It was rusty, not used for its original purpose in some time. It squeaked and whined as it went.

The boy, just a teenager, riding on the flat top tried to move, to wriggle free, but the thick straps around his arms and legs, across his waist and chest, stopped even the slightest of movements.

He tried to yell out, to scream for help. Surely there must be someone close who could help him.

He wanted to move his head, to rave about his situation.

Again, he could not; the strap across his forehead stopped this also. He could feel the dirty rag jammed into his mouth starting to creep down his throat, and he could taste the bile starting to rise up his gullet.

He kept it down with sheer force of will.

The boy had no idea how he had gotten there. One moment he had been partying with friends, when he had stepped outside for some much-needed fresh air. After that...nothing.

His clothes, shoes, and wallet were gone. Now, all he had left were the boxers he wore.

The trolley continued down the corridor.

Above him, he could make out the shape of light globes. Those that weren't broken gave out a dim light that strobed his eyes as he passed underneath. All around him, the walls and ceiling were cracked with zig-zagging lines. It was obvious to him, even in his state, that wherever he was had not been used for some time.

The trolley crashed through strips of thick plastic, the type that were hung in butcher's freezers, and his heart started to beat faster. He was wheeled a little farther and then was stopped. He heard the brakes on the wheels go on.

Someone moved around one side and his eyes widened in horror. He would have opened his mouth and screamed if he could. The man was shirtless. He wore a blood-stained butcher's apron over his muscled torso. His arms were covered in coarse black hair. He was big; not tall big...but footballer big. Huge, imposing...somehow brutal-looking like a Neanderthal.

There was a mask on his face, and this is what made him want to scream. The flesh was old, he could tell that much. It looked like a tanned piece of leather. Black eyes, reflecting the light like a shark, stared out from behind the covering. The lips had been stitched shut with a series of tight crosses, the ends dangled from knots at either end. His head was shaved bald and he could see a sheen of sweat on the shorn dome.

The man picked up an IV needle and plunged it into his arm, just below the crook of his elbow. After this was done, the mountain of a man stepped back. He saw the tube run from his arm to an upturned, hanging bottle of something above his head.

Footsteps echoed in the space, but with his head tied, he couldn't see where they were coming from.

They came closer; the sound of heeled shoes on tile.

"Is he ready?"

A grunt of readiness from beside him. A smooth hand, a man's hand, reached down and undid the clasp holding down his head. He didn't want to look, but he knew he had to. Lifting his head, he looked at where he had been brought.

There was another figure in the room with them now. They had their back to him, so he couldn't see a face.

This individual wore a dark blue suit and, as he watched, pulled a pristine apron over his head and fastened it around his waist. He reached down and picked up a mask from a table, placing it over his face.

Then he turned around.

Steve looked back at him; his friend of the last ten years...or rather, the stitched-together face of Steve did so. It looked like it had been cut from his friend's head and stitched back together; the lines of tight staples, making it a patchwork of ruined skin. Fresh blood still seeped from around the edges.

The man stepped over to him and reached up to the bottle, slowly adjusting the flow.

The boy felt a rush of ice hit his veins, his heart starting to beat slower. His limbs felt leaden and heavy.

He was sure he would be unable to move them even if he wasn't tied down. His eyes opened and he managed to suck in a breath past the gag.

"There," the voice purred. "That's better. We wouldn't want you to miss the show."

Turning once more, he reached for a camera set up on a tripod and pressed a button. A red light blinked in readiness. A laptop sat nearby and he pushed the power button.

He stepped back and spread his arms wide.

"Ladies and gentlemen... Welcome to tonight's auction."

Mac was late, he was going to miss it. He jumped out of the truck, leaving his keys in the ignition, and ran into the house. The front door swung shut at his back. He wondered what would be on offer tonight.

His mouth started to fill with saliva at the thought. It was getting harder to get fresh meat these days, but hopefully he could grab a bargain this evening.

He put his wallet on the counter, making sure he could grab his credit card if he needed it, and opened his laptop. Good, he hadn't missed much.

Dr. Stanforth sat in his padded chair in his office and watched the man as he pranced about on the screen. He shook his head but didn't turn off the computer.

He needed fresh organs for his experiments, and the donors were few and far between. The young man on the gurney looked healthy enough. Maybe tonight would be his lucky night.

Reed Smith ushered his last customer out the door and flicked the latch. Reaching up, he spun the sign to closed and pulled the blinds. Retreating back behind the desk, he lifted the tablet from underneath.

The boss didn't know he had it at work, and wouldn't be pleased if he knew it was there. He didn't use it often, but tonight was special.

He wasn't buying today, but it never hurt to look.

Brad always gave him a little extra if he was able to goose the prices a little.

All across the land, in homes and offices, people turned on devices—tablets and computers—to watch and to buy.

"So. I see we have our regular bidders here tonight, and some new names. To everyone...welcome."

He turned and nodded at the bigger man, who lifted a meat cleaver in one of his beefy hands. He walked over to the boy and stood over him.

"Let's start with an appetizer, shall we? What am I to bid for this juicy, meaty leg? You know what you have to do. Start the clock."

The stained blade lowered and stopped just above his foot.

The other man looked back at the computer screen.

"No? You want more, do you?"

The steel moved up his leg to just below his knee. That brought a response from whoever was online. Monetary amounts started to come in thick and fast, the numbers on the screen ticking ever upwards. A bell sounded, and the man checked the screen.

"Congratulations, ghoul130. This is for you."

A nod...the lifting and falling of the cleaver.

The razor edge bit into the meat just below his left knee, the pain huge and blinding. Pulled from his leg, it fell again and again. It chopped through the bones in his leg with splintering cracks, the large man sawing backwards and forwards, cutting through veins and muscle, flesh and fat. He opened his mouth and screamed, the noise bouncing around the tiled room as the gag fell from his mouth.

The lower leg came free and thumped onto the top of the wheeled trolley. The butcher lifted it and placed it in a box filled with ice. He closed the lid.

The boy's eyes streamed with tears, snot dribbling from his nose and over his lips. He wanted to plead, to beg, but the words stuck in his throat and would not come. He watched with shock as the man tied off the leg. The bleeding slowed but didn't stop.

"Better fix that," the auctioneer said.

The butcher picked up a cook's blowtorch and flicked it on. He passed the blue flame across the stump of the leg, searing the wound. Flesh started to crisp, small wisps of smoke drifting from the cooking meat. The boy smelled BBQ and realized that he was smelling himself as he cooked. The man went back to stand before the camera again.

"Now that we have things going, why don't we offer something bigger?"

The boy watched, horrified that he was still conscious, as the big man put down the cleaver and picked up a bone saw. He moved to stand up by his shoulder.

People obviously knew what was about to happen, the bids rolling in already. Again the bell sounded, and the man rubbed his hands together. He nodded his head.

"The left arm, if you would."

The toothed edge of the saw was lowered and pushed down into the meat between his shoulder and neck.

It started to move.

The pain was worse than he could have imagined. His head rocked from side to side as the blade cut through the skin and into the bone underneath. His screams were high-pitched, hoarse with suffering.

Why was he still conscious? He should be dead from shock at the very least, yet still he continued to stay awake and aware.

The surgical saw made short work of the bones and tendons of his shoulder. One last push and the toothed edge cut into the thin, blood-soaked mattress he lay on. He was aware that he had soiled himself; the smell of piss and shit hanging in the air. The smaller man moved further away, but it didn't seem to affect the bigger butcher.

As he had done before, he lifted the severed arm and put it into a cold case, closing the lid. The auctioneer stepped closer, wafting a hand in front of his face. He looked into the boy's eyes, at his pale color. Then he looked up to the bottle connected to the IV tube. He walked back to his spot.

"It looks like we have time for one more auction, folks." He nodded his head slowly. "Unfortunately, they don't keep fresh for long." He uttered a small giggle.

"So, I am going to offer the organs as a one-time offer. Start your bidding now, please."

Once more the numbers on the screen started to climb. They went slowly at first, but rapidly increased. Soon only two numbers were still rising. The bell rang and the counters stopped. The auctioneer clapped, happy at the amount.

The butcher went to work.

The boy on the trolley watched as the big man ran a knife along his stomach, the thin line of red starting to run faster and faster. The blade cut a horizontal line across and then a longer one from just below his throat down to his navel. With one huge hand, he peeled the skin and flaps of muscle to the sides. He dropped the knife and lifted a pair of curved steel shears.

The boy's movements were weaker now, his strength starting to fade with everything that was being done to him. A line of bright red blood slipped from the corner of his mouth and dripped to the sheet under his head.

The small blades grabbed hold of his ribs and, with the big man's arms flexing, cut through them one after the other. The butcher dropped the shears and grabbed the edges of the ribcage, slowly and carefully lifting it away. He dropped it on top of the tray full of tools.

A smaller pair of snips was picked up, looking delicate in his hands, and he went to work. One at a time, the organs were cut through and placed in small, travel-sized ice boxes. It was as he cut through the veins holding the kidneys in place that the boy lapsed into blessed unconsciousness.

As the last of the bottles fluid drained into his system, his heart was laboring to beat. It slowed, slowed... stopped, as the big man pulled it from his chest and placed it into an icebox with the rest of his insides.

The auctioneer turned to the camera.

"I'm afraid that's all she wrote, folks." He gestured to the remains of the body. "The rest will of course be offered at a reduced rate. Not as fresh as while the blood is still flowing. But I am sure someone will be after a bargain." He held up a finger. "However, the head and skin will not be included. Join us next week for more great deals."

He reached out and turned off the camera. He pulled off the flesh mask covering his face with the other, taking a deep breath. He turned to face the big butcher.

"Take the head and send it with the organs, please. I'm sure the buyer would appreciate the gesture." He knew that Stanforth, one of his longest-running buyers, would like the head for his experiments. He was one sick bastard. He smiled to himself.

"Skin what's left, then get rid of it."

The big man grunted and nodded, setting to work. As the auctioneer walked away, he could hear the whine of a bone saw as it powered up.

The skin would be stretched and cured, aged until it looked like tanned leather. It was amazing how some people still didn't know what their goods were made of. He had made wallets, purses, and even rebound old books in the dermis. The shop he owned at the campsite was making some good money. He made sure his suit was still unmarked and walked out into the halls of the abandoned building. He must remember to give Reed a little extra for jacking up the price at the end. He would have known the doctor would be all over those organs.

Mac let out a sigh and smiled as he closed the laptop and leaned back. The meat in his freezer was getting low and he was glad he had managed to secure some more.

The site on the dark web had been the best place to satisfy his 'desires.' Chopping up people was getting riskier these days. He knew that his purchase would be delivered to the same place at the same time within 24 hours. He had enough to last that long.

It had cost him an arm and a leg, but he was happy.

He started to giggle, his shoulders shaking as he realized his little joke.

Dr. Stanforth shut off his computer and poured himself a glass of ten-year-old scotch.

He had paid more than he had wanted to, but it would be worth it to have the organs.

People were willing to pay any amount for good black-market replacements. He would make his money back threefold.

All he had to do now was wait for his delivery to reach him.

Reed turned off the tablet and stashed it back under the counter. He grinned, knowing he would make some good bank from this. Brad would see him right.

He stood up and flipped the sign back to open, unlocking the door at the same time.

He saw a car pull up to the pumps and a man get out. He ran through the rain towards him. He could see a woman sleeping in the passenger seat.

The door opened and the man came inside, shaking his jacket on the floor.

"Evening," Reed said, his tone friendly and welcoming.

"Uh, hi...sorry about the floor."

Reed waved a hand. "No problem, I was about to sweep anyway. Help you with something?"

The man pulled a waterlogged map from his pocket and started to unfold it.

"My sat nav crapped out on me; I don't know how the old folks managed to get around." He smiled and Reed returned the look.

"There are some cabins around here somewhere? Trying to get away from the world for a while."

Reed leaned over the map and jabbed a finger down.

"That's where you want to go, friend. Just keep going west. You'll see the turnoff; can't miss it."

The man put the mess of paper back in a pocket and held out a hand. "Thank you, very kind."

He turned and, lifting his collar against the rain, stepped back outside. Reed watched as he went, his hand reaching into a pocket of his overalls to pull his cell out. Without looking, he dialed a number that he knew by heart.

It rang once...twice. A voice on the other end.

"Hey brother, what are you like for inventory? Have a couple more that you may want to take a look at." He listened for a second, nodding his head.

"Sent them your way, should see them soon."

He rang off and put the phone back in his pocket.

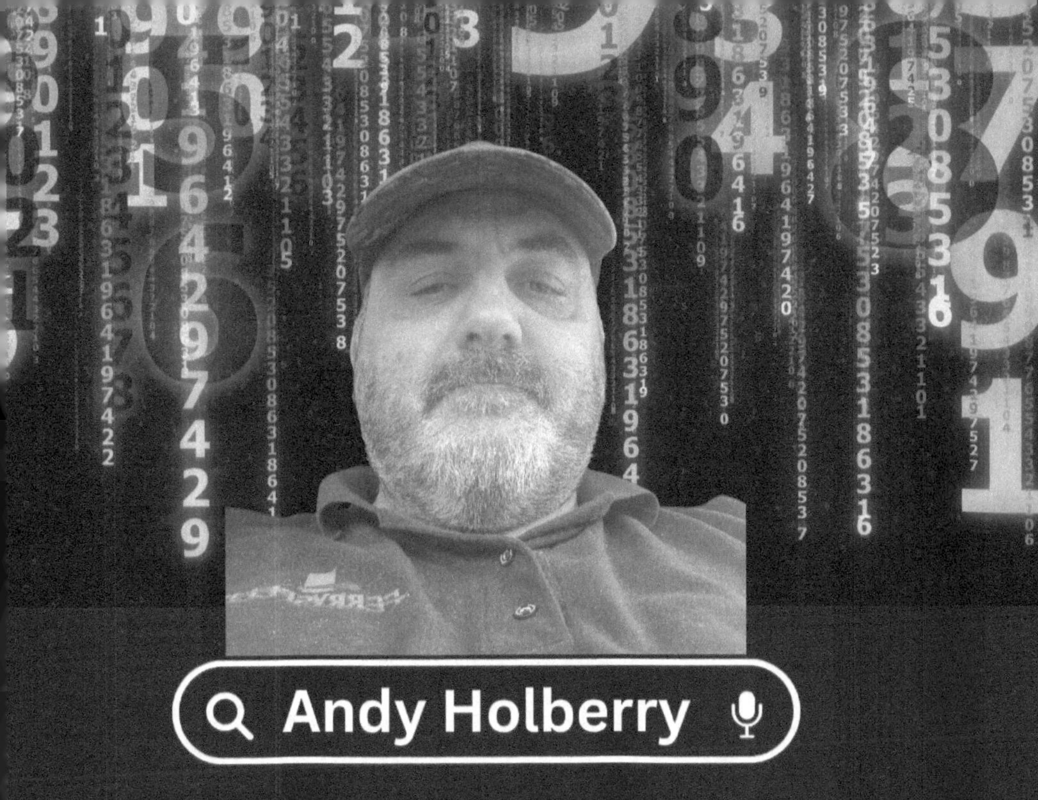

Andy Holberry heralds from an island that no one has heard of just south of one of the busiest shipping lanes in the world. Author of the zombie cruiseship thriller "Voyage," he loves to write and read...a lot.
His favorite authors are Guy Smith, James Herbert, and Stephen King. If some people are to be believed, he is part robot-- and he's good with that!

Chapter 4

The Ritual

Rian Burnhouse

The faded, wooden sign creaked on its chains as the ocean breeze swept through the mismatched buildings of Dirk's Landing. What had her mother seen in this place? There was nothing for her to do. Even though it was a beach town, the dreary New England weather kept it too cold to enjoy.

The constant, clammy wind cut right through her corseted blouse. From the looks that the old women coming out of the general store gave her, it seemed that her outfit was having the desired effect. There were only a few hundred people in this town, and half of those were as old and dilapidated as the two dozen squat buildings that comprised "downtown." Anyone with an ounce of style would turn heads in this hovel.

She doffed her bag as she entered through the ill-fitting front door of their Victorian home. The stairs squealed in protest as she made her way up to her room.

"Is that you, Carmine?" her mom's airy voice called from the parlor, where she spent most of her time. She would never understand why people paid so much money for her mom's soulless landscape pieces.

Who the hell else would it be?

"Yes, mother." She failed to keep her voice from sounding condescending.

Once in her room, she felt the tension drain from her shoulders, seeing the only thing that brought her any solace in this desolate town. The sound of her computer booting up drowned out the constant whistle of the wind through this ramshackle house. Custom-made headphones snuggled her ears, separating her from this placid world. To many people, her music would instill thoughts of mania or anxiety, but for her, metal brought on a sense of calm and peacefulness.

Carmine had no agenda on this jaunt through the internet-verse; she just wanted to be away from Dirk's Landing. What began with social media quickly moved on to darker things. Her affinity for the macabre often led her into the darker corners of the internet, and this evening was no different.

The sun crawled its way down the sky to hide behind the horizon, leaving her in a dark room lit only by the blue glow of her computer screen. Carmine didn't notice—she was tumbling down a rabbit hole of occult practices and ancient rituals. A few minutes into her deep dive on whether there were still cultures that performed human sacrifices, she had a message pop up on her screen.

"Find what you're looking for?" it read.

What the hell? She had no idea how one of these fake help messages had gotten through her spam blocker. She realized in a moment that she didn't know which messaging software sent it. She minimized the window and looked through her computer's installed programs, and there it was; *Ghostspeech.* She hadn't installed that.

Dammit, Mom. I told you not to touch my computer; your phone can do all the trivial tasks you need. After deleting the unwanted software, she tried to pick up where she left off, but a thought kept nagging at the back of her mind—her mom doesn't know how to install things.

Bing!

There it was again. She was on a completely different website, and there was the little window. Except this time it read, "You don't want to ignore me."

"Or you'll start the singularity?" she typed, then erased it. She wasn't going to waste her time talking to a bot.

"No," it responded. "Or you'll miss out on the thing you've been craving."

Okay, at this point it probably wasn't a bot. And it was definitely viewing her screen somehow because it responded to a message she hadn't sent. She checked her installed programs again, and there it was; *Ghostspeech*. She had dabbled with hacking enough to know that whoever this was, they were good.

"Alright, perv! What exactly do you think I've been craving?" she typed.

It wrote a one-word reply, "Acceptance."

"Alright, what do you want?" she typed. "I'm a rich billionaire, and I'll give you anything to leave me alone."

"No, you're not," it responded. "You're a teenage girl from Dirk's Landing."

Be cool, she told herself, *he can't hurt you through the internet. You don't have friends he can turn against you, and you don't even have a bank account.*

"Alright, cool guy, with your fancy computer in your mom's basement, what DO you want?" she typed.

"To help you," it wrote.

"No, thanks," she wrote. "I will commence ignoring you now."

"Instead, how would you like to see something you've never seen before?" it wrote.

"Sir or madam, I've got an onion router. I've seen things that would make your nerdy knees weak," she wrote.

"Through a monitor, from the safety of your mother's house," it wrote. Then a montage of every image of her and every search she'd ever typed showed up, even the ones from her incognito tab. Her mom would have a heart attack if she saw a tenth of what was on this screen. "I can show you visceral things IRL."

The thought of an internet predator finding her when she was on this side of the internet had always been there, but this was not what she had expected. What would it hurt to give in to curiosity a little bit and at least find out what this dork thought was "visceral"?

"First, tell me what to call you, as you clearly already know my name. Then, maybe I'll listen to what you have to say," she typed.

"Call me opportunity," it wrote.

"TELL ME, OR THIS CONVERSATION IS OVER!" she typed.

"SECT" it typed.

"Carmine!" her mother's voice called sharply from behind her.

She quickly exited out of all the windows she had open. Her mom couldn't handle all of this.

"Yes, mother?" Carmine said, feigning innocence as she spun her chair around.

Her mom's stern visage softened. "Being eighteen doesn't mean you can do whatever you want. You need to be more responsible. It's after midnight, and you have school tomorrow."

"Sorry, mother," Carmine responded. It was no use arguing with her. With the amount of medication she was on, she would probably forget this conversation ever happened, anyway.

Carmine gave her mother enough time to get to her room, and a few extra minutes for her "nighttime" medication to take effect. The house was quiet, so she scrambled back over to her computer.

Sect had sent several messages that she scanned half-heartedly. The last of these read, "This is what we do," and included a link.

The link led her to a virtual recreation of a real place, like on GPS street view images. She could move her viewpoint around. It was dimly lit, but she could make out the surroundings. She was facing the inside of a shed's door. As she slid her mouse around, the angle of the room she was viewing changed. After turning completely around, she was met with a horrible, beautiful, grotesque scene.

Several red candles sputtered around the room, nearing the end of their short lives. Slumped against the far wall was the gutted form of a young woman, her intestines spilled in her lap. On the floor, in a small metal bowl, was the remnant of something that had been burned. A thought struck Carmine—she had seen this earlier in her research. This is how ancient Romans had sacrificed vestal virgins that had broken their vows. That meant only one thing could be in that brazier: the girl's heart.

"Holy shit!" she said out loud in her room.

"What do you think?" Sect typed.

Be cool. She had seen horrible things before. He couldn't phase her. "Seems sloppy," she wrote.

"You think you can do better?" Sect wrote.

What the hell did that mean? There was no way she could do something like that, she didn't want him to know that, though. "Of course I could," she wrote.

"Prove it. Our group just so happens to have a recent opening, and we want to see if you have what it takes to join," Sect wrote.

His next message contained three names, names that she recognized. One was a girl from school, April Walker. The second, Oscar Dell, was a weirdo who worked at the hardware store in town that always looked at her a little bit too long. The last name caused her heart to jump into her throat. It was her mother's. "These are approved candidates," he wrote.

Yeah, this stuff intrigued her, even excited her, but she wasn't going to hurt anyone. The time for being cool was over.

"I'm sorry, I can't," she wrote.

"If you don't, someone else will," he wrote.

Shit! Did he mean that someone else would hurt one of these three people? Her heart was pounding in her ears. She wasn't a huge fan of her mother, but she didn't want her to die. April had always seemed sweet, though she'd never really talked to her. That guy from the hardware store, well, if she had to pick one...

"Okay, I'll do it," she wrote. This was insane.

"You have until sunrise," Sect wrote. "Message from your phone when it's done. We have a representative in the area who will verify your work." The window closed, and a progress bar popped up as *Ghostspeech* uninstalled itself.

Carmine pushed her chair back from her desk and sucked in a deep breath. What the hell had she gotten herself into? She pulled out her phone to check the time; it was just a little after 2:00 a.m. Sunrise was in a few hours. There was no other choice. If she didn't want her mom or April to get hurt, she had to do something, something bad.

It was no trouble sneaking out without her mom knowing. That lady could sleep through a hurricane after taking her pills. Carmine wasn't proud of it, but she had momentarily considered what an easy target her mom would've been. She could never hurt her own mother. At least she could convince herself that Oscar might even deserve it. Just being around him made her uncomfortable.

The hardware store seemed like the obvious place to start. She would kill two birds with one stone. His address had to be there somewhere, and there were supplies there that she could use.

Crossing the barren streets of Dirk's Landing proved much easier than avoiding detection when she had snuck out back in her old town. She kept to the shadows, but there were only a couple of cops in this town. Even still, she went to the back door of the hardware store. Picking locks was a skill she had mastered when she was still in middle school. She had since moved on to bigger and better things, but the skill came in useful from time to time. In just a moment, she was inside.

Beams of moonlight drove spears through the woody dust that permeated the main room of the hardware store. A quick search of the office yielded what she was here for. She plugged Oscar's address into her phone. He lived just outside of town, on a lonely little road that ran along the shore. It didn't look like there were any other houses near his. Perfect.

As she grabbed some supplies from the tools section, she saw lights outside. A lone patrol car went by, windows down, country music blaring. Even if she hadn't ducked, he would have been oblivious to her.

A brand-new pack, stuffed with tools for her coming trial, bounced against her back as she jogged out of town. To avoid any more police, she headed through the woods up the hill towards Oscar's house.

A lone, mournful howl sounded in the distance. She didn't know there were wolves in this area. It sounded pained. It sounded lost. It sounded lonely. It sounded like the bitter note of her own soul. Without a thought as to why, she tossed her head back and blasted as heartfelt a howl as she could muster. There, hopefully the wolf didn't feel as alone as she did anymore.

Oscar's house stood on the edge of a cliff overlooking the cold Atlantic Ocean. Up here, the wind was even stronger than it was in the town below. By the dilapidated state of his house, it seemed he was lucky that the wind hadn't knocked it down.

As she crossed the porch, the creak of every board seemed to reverberate up her spine. Hopefully he was as sound a sleeper as her mother was. A thought came to her for the first time: What if he fought back? How had she not considered this sooner? She had all the supplies she needed for after the deed was done, but how would she go about the first part, the killing part?

Something in her bag would have to do. She peered through the front window. It was a living room that looked like it belonged in an Edgar Allan Poe story, complete with a fireplace and lush, wingback chairs. Sitting in the chair, facing somewhat towards the window, was Oscar. His head rested against the side of his oversized chair, a half dozen pill bottles on the table next to him. Maybe he was like her mom and this might be easier than she thought.

Even still, she circled around to look for a back door. Her stomach lurched, being this close to the edge of the cliff. The wind howled in her ears. Between her stop by the hardware store and her trip through the woods, it was past 4:00 a.m. She could see the faintest pale light starting to spread along the horizon on the water. She didn't have a lot of time left.

The old lock on the back door was a lot stiffer than the one at the hardware store, but after a few minutes, she was able to force the lock to turn. Every step she took sounded like a thunder crack in the house's deathly silence. The hallway inside the door led straight through the middle of the house, from the front door to the back, with a stairway leading up on one side.

The entrance to the living room was past the stairs on the right. The flickering of the dying fire cast splashes of orange light into the hallway. With the help of his pills, hopefully he would be right where she left him. When she was a foot from the frame of the open doorway that led into the living room, she heard the distinct creaking of old springs. He was getting up from his chair.

Carmine froze. He would surely hear her if she retreated, but if he came out here...

She listened intently to his footsteps. He took only three, but they didn't sound any closer.

"There you go, that's better," Oscar said in a soft, gentle tone.

Who was he talking to? Carmine couldn't contain her curiosity. One eye was all that she dared peek around the frame. He was bent, holding a glass of water so that an elderly woman could drink. She moaned quietly.

"I know you don't like it, Ma," Oscar whispered quietly, stroking her silver hair. "But the doctor says you have to take these, and I'm not ready to lose you." Carmine gasped involuntarily, and pulled herself back from the doorway.

"Who's there?" Oscar called.

She heard a metallic scrape, "Get out!" he called. "I don't want to have to hurt you."

What was she going to do? He didn't deserve this, but she doubted April did, either. His footsteps stalked slowly towards her as he continued to shout warnings. She looked down the hall, out the still-open back door. The sky was painted with shades of pink now. Even if she wanted to pick someone else, there wasn't enough time. He was almost to her now. She needed to run.

No, she wouldn't let someone hurt her mom. She dug in her bag, desperately searching as he came around the corner. He held the fire poker like a baseball bat, ready to swing. The determination in his eyes softened to concern as he saw her cowered there. He began to lower his makeshift weapon.

"Carmine? What are you do—" His words were drowned out as she blasted him with the fire extinguisher she had taken from the hardware store. The fire poker crashed to the floor.

He gouged at his eyes, gagging and spitting out mouthfuls of foam. "What kind of prank are you pulling?" he said. As Carmine raised her weapon, she saw his eyes finally come back into focus.

"Put the knife down," he said, holding his hands out towards her in a calming gesture. "I'm sure whatever is going on, we can work it out."

Tears welled in her eyes. She gripped her knife so tightly that the ridges of the handle dug into her hand, and her knuckles turned white. "You don't understand," she said.

"I want to understand," he replied. He was walking slowly towards her, still trying to calm her down.

She backed slowly away from him, knife still raised. "Back up!" she screamed. "It's either you or them."

"Everything is going to be okay," he said. He was still advancing, and she was still retreating. They were almost to the back door.

"One more step, Oscar, and I'll do it," she growled, gesturing with the knife.

He continued steadily forward as he said, "Let's just talk ab—"

She drove the knife towards his chest. He reacted quickly, and caught her wrist. She reached up with her other hand, trying to force the knife down. His other hand clasped on her throat and slammed her into the wall. He was so strong.

"Why are you doing this?" he said through gritted teeth. "What did I do to you?"

She couldn't breathe with his callused hand threatening to crush her throat. Darkness crowded in at the edges of her vision. If she didn't think of something, she would pass out. Who knew what Sect would do after that? Her knee came crashing up between his legs, crushing his manhood.

His grip released, and she eagerly gulped down the cool morning air. He clutched at his privates as he crumpled to the ground.

Tears ran down her cheeks as she stalked towards him, "I'm so, so sorry," she said. "I wish there was another way."

She fell upon him, knife driving towards his heart. He rolled to the side, and she jammed the knife deep into his shoulder. He grabbed her, and they rolled, a tumbling ball of flesh, blood, and fire extinguisher foam. As they scrambled, she bit and clawed at him, doing whatever damage she could. He finally got so that he was half on top of her, then reached up to grip the handle of the knife protruding from his shoulder. With one firm yank, he pulled it free.

"Why?" he asked again. He was crying now, too. He raised the knife above his head, preparing a powerful, overhead stab.

"NO!" Carmine screamed as she kicked him back off of her. He dropped the knife as he was launched backwards. Surprise washed across his face as he realized that he had run out of ground.

"Why?" he begged one last time as he groped at the empty air, toppled over the ledge, and was gone. He didn't even scream on the way down.

Carmine crawled over to the edge and looked down. There was nothing left of him that she could see, other than a large red swath of water that was lapping against the jagged rocks.

The rim of the sun was just peeking over the horizon, sprinkling the sea with a beautiful cascade of orange and red light. Carmine spared a moment to think about how beautiful the world could be and understood, for the first time, the value in her mother's work. She snapped back to reality. Time was up, and she had failed to set up a proper sacrifice. There was no way she could make it to one of the other proposed victims before Sect took matters into his own hands.

Then a horrible, insidious, wonderful idea crept into her brain. It was a long shot, but maybe they would accept a replacement.

Carmine rose, straightened her clothes, and walked back up the hallway, scooping up her bag of supplies as she went.

"Good morning, Mrs. Dell," she said, entering the quiet living room, all the emotion gone from her voice.

When her gruesome work was done, she pulled out her phone. Carmine was not surprised to find the *Ghostspeech* app already downloaded on it, her conversation with Sect open and waiting.

"It's done," she typed, followed by Oscar's address. She stepped back to admire her work. This piece was modeled after descriptions she had read about an ancient African tribe's tradition. After killing Oscar, this part had actually been easier than she had expected, almost enjoyable.

A few short minutes later, there was a knock at the door. It was a pretty girl, older than her, but not by much. Carmine had the strange sensation that she had seen her somewhere before.

"Creepy house, great touch," she said. She sounded excited, giddy even. "I had no idea you were into this stuff!"

Carmine showed her to the living room, where her masterpiece was on display.

"Oh, wow," she said, moving over to the corpse. She ran two fingers through Mrs. Dell's blood. "It looks so real," she said and stuck her fingers in her mouth. "Ugh, it tastes awful, that's not cranberries. What did you use for the blood?"

Carmine could feel every hair on her body standing up. Her brain was shuttering back through the memories of the last several hours, and she remembered where she had seen this girl. Out of context, she hadn't recognized her. It was April Walker, but it was also the girl from the virgin sacrifice that Sect had shown her.

How was she alive, and what did she have to do with this?

"It's real," Carmine whispered.

"What?" April said.

"IT'S REAL!" Carmine screamed. "Isn't this what you people wanted? 'If I didn't do it, someone else would,' that's what Sect said."

April looked mortified, "S.E.C.T. is the name of the group we wanted you to join: The Special Effects Cosmetics Tribunal."

Carmine looked down at her blood-covered hands. How had she done this? She was going to be in big trouble if anyone found out. April stared at her. The look on her face was undeniable; there was no way she was going to keep this a secret.

Carmine glanced to the side, where her bloody knife lay on a table between them. April quickly realized what Carmine was thinking. She lunged for the knife, but Carmine was quicker.

On her way home, she kept to the woods as far as she could, to hide her blood-soaked clothes. When she reached her house, it was well past sunrise, and her mother would be up by now. Going through the front door wouldn't work. Her mother always heard her come in from her parlor.

Carmine attempted to climb up the trellis to go in through her bedroom window. The cool ocean breeze chilled the sweat on her neck and face, the first time she had been thankful for that relentless wind. A few tense moments of climbing, and she was through the window, dropping onto the floor of her bedroom. She was safe. There was enough time to get cleaned up and leave for school without her mom knowing a thing.

She struggled to her feet, her legs burning from the hike. Then she noticed her mother was sitting straight-backed on the edge of her bed. "Where the hell—" she started, but gasped in surprise as she noticed all the blood. "Carmine!" she shrieked, rushing over to her. "Who did this? Where are you bleeding from? I'll call an ambulance!" She was speaking so quickly that all her words were running together. She had her phone out.

"No, Mom, don't call an ambulance," Carmine said.

"Whatever happened to you, it's not your fault, baby. You didn't do anything wrong," her mother said. She was dialing now.

"Mom, stop!" Carmine shouted. Then said more calmly, "It's not my blood."

"What do you mean, it's not yours?" her mother asked. "You're delirious. Sit down."

"No, I'm not. They were going to hurt you. I had to do something," Carmine said.

"What did you do?" she said.

Carmine didn't respond.

Her mother's face morphed from concern to fear, speckled with anger. "What did you do?" she said more aggressively.

Carmine just shook her head, looking down at her blood-covered blouse.

"What did you do?" Her mother's voice was barely a whisper now.

Carmine looked up. She saw exactly what she had expected in her mother's face. It was the same look that April had given her, the same look Oscar had right before the end. There was only one thing to do; her fingers curled around the handle of the knife in her pack. At least she would get to finish the list.

Rian Burnhouse is a lifelong fan of fantasy novels, which has translated into a love for writing his own fantasy works and creating Dungeons & Dragons content for his quickly growing YouTube channel. He is currently writing his first novel while growing his fan base as "Dad the Dungeon Master" on YouTube. He spends his free time enjoying his family, writing short stories, and running tabletop games for his friends and YT followers.

Chapter 5
Rage of the Bobcat

Bill Freas

Barbara hacked raucously until she was finally able to bring up the nagging glob of dark mucus that had her gagging and choking for almost twenty minutes.

Mornings were the worst for her, but at least she had the care and support of her loyal, loving daughter, Arielle. The 27-year-old juggled the arduous day-to-day task of caring for her chronically ill mother, with the long, thankless hours of employment as a low-level nurse at a hospital in the city.

Fortunately, she had some help from a reliable visiting aide whose services were only partially covered by her mom's Medicare insurance. The circumstances were quite stressful and financially straining, but Arielle forged through it all like a workhorse saint. No mother on Earth could have asked for a better daughter than her.

It was early on a cool, cloudy Tuesday morning when the health advisor from Barbara's doctor's office came to their home to talk to Arielle before she headed off into the city for her next nursing shift. The advisor was a serious but caring woman who addressed things bluntly.

"She's hanging in there. Every day... is a challenge, but we'll get through it," Arielle said to the woman in a private chat in the kitchen.

"Is she using her oscillation vest?" the advisor asked.

Arielle nodded assuredly. "Three times a day. More, if necessary."

"Good. Cystic fibrosis isn't something to treat lightly. The vest and her regimen of meds are the only ways to keep her stable right now," the advisor explained.

"Well, you're a nurse. You know. I don't have to tell you this. Sorry, it's just habit, I guess."

Arielle smiled understandingly before the advisor addressed another major concern.

"There is the glaring financial matter of continuing her treatments and the new meds Dr. Simes prescribed for her recently—not to mention the cost of the visiting health aide. Your mom's supplemental insurance isn't even coming close to covering the co-pays and other costs that Medicare won't touch. Her out-of-pocket balance for all of this is reaching about $75,000, Arielle. In six more months, it'll be over a hundred grand. Unfortunately, our office can't keep accepting the bare-bones minimum you and your mom have been paying toward her balance. I hate delivering this news to you, but if they don't get another two hundred a month, they'll put the account into collections and refer your mom to an in-patient, long-term Medicaid facility."

Arielle's stomach dropped, and her face flushed with anxiety. "A state clinic? You know how those places are run. My mom wouldn't last a year in one of those."

The advisor sighed. "I know they're not the most ideal spots to send a loved one. You soon may not have a choice, though, Arielle."

"The bills are piling up here," Arielle replied. "Two hundred more a month is next to impossible. I don't know what else to do,"

Hopelessness was settling into her home, and there wasn't any tangible relief in sight.

The tavern was crowded, but Arielle and three of her nursing colleagues of similar age—Emma, Rosy, and

Greg—managed to slip in after their long shift for a quick evening drink to unwind. It was a rare moment of fun and relaxation for Arielle, in particular. Four shot glasses of tequila were raised into the air at their table near a corner of the room.

"Here's to shorter shifts, better pay, and hotter patients," Emma toasted.

"Cheers!" the others exclaimed as they tapped glasses and then threw back their shots.

"Damn, either I'm getting old, or this stuff is getting stronger," Greg said, wincing from the tequila's wallop.

"Wimp," Rosy replied.

"After today, I think I'm gonna need, like, eight more of these... at least," Emma added.

Arielle forced a grin at the banter, but her closest friend of the bunch, Emma, could tell that there was worry bubbling under the surface.

"Hey, you okay?" she asked Arielle quietly while Rosy and Greg chatted with each other.

Arielle nodded. "Yeah, I'm good."

"Nah, I know you too well. Nine years and counting. Speak now, or forever hold my hair back when I vomit after future gluttonous happy hours."

Tears welling up in her eyes, Arielle hesitated and then confessed to her good friend. "It's my mom's bills. Things are getting out of control, Em. Every day feels like quicksand."

"I'm so sorry, hon. If I had the money, you know I..."

Arielle touched her friend's hand gratefully before she could finish the kind thought.

Fate then stepped in, and Arielle locked eyes with a handsome young man across the room. He was standing at the bar, drinking leisurely with a couple of friends of his own. Arielle couldn't break the stare with him. It was an instant connection, and it was magnetic.

Emma noticed this and smirked with sly encouragement. "That there might at least help you get your mind off things for a while."

Arielle blushed, unable to hold back her own slippery grin. The feeling pulsed from head to toe—a natural pleasure she hadn't felt in a long time.

A full hour had passed since Arielle's friends had left the tavern. Arielle stayed behind, joining the engaging young man in an adjacent booth, the two getting to know each other and feeling out this amazing spark. His name was Jansen, and he was a charming gentleman, unlike many of the men Arielle encountered daily, especially in the city. He was intelligent, thoughtful, confident, and respectful—just the elixir Arielle needed during this trying time in her life.

"You're my new hero," he said.

Arielle smiled and looked away shyly.

"No, I'm serious. Nurse by day... and night sometimes. And taking care of your mom and your home, and not angry or bitter or resentful of it all. Most people in your shoes would turn bad or go crazy. You're an incredible, inspiring woman. I hope you see that when you look in the mirror," he said.

"That's really sweet. Some days, I do feel like I'm on the brink of going crazy. But I love my mom. She was there for me my whole life—the good times and the really, really tough times. I would swim the Nile for her. I just wish, financially, we didn't have to struggle the way we are, y'know?"

He nodded sympathetically while slowly swirling the straw in his nearly empty glass of gin and tonic. There was a tired pause in the conversation before she spotted a tattoo peeking out from below his shirt collar, near the top of his left pectoral muscle.

"What kind of ink you got tucked in there?" Arielle inquired playfully.

He glanced down at his tattoo and chuckled. "Oh, this?"

She nodded as he gently pulled down his shirt collar, revealing the head of a spotted, gray and brown creature with golden eyes.

"Wow, is that a wolf?" she asked.

"Bobcat. The king of the forest."

"Very cool design."

He gazed at his ink admiringly. "Yeah, thanks. It symbolizes an inner strength that's vital to me. The power and dominance of the bobcat. It's a creed that fuels my spirit."

Arielle truly appreciated his poignant and profound viewpoint. It was rare for her to meet someone with such depth, someone who contributed more than the mundane.

They finished their drinks and headed out to the quiet parking lot, where the cool night breeze danced on their warm skin. Both turned bashful and exchanged nervous small talk on the way to Arielle's car.

"Thanks for walking me to my car," she said. "Are you parked close by?"

"Sure thing. I'm only a few rows over. You okay to drive home?"

"All good," she replied. "Water does the trick every time."

Again, there was an awkward pause until Jansen found his courage.

"Would it... be okay if I called you sometime?"

Arielle grinned sincerely. "Yeah... I'd like that."

They exchanged phones and entered their numbers into each other's contacts. After they handed back their respective phones, Jansen leaned in and gave Arielle a soft, polite peck on the cheek.

"I had a great time tonight, Arielle," he said before turning away and sauntering off with a new pep in his step and his hands tucked casually into his jacket pockets.

She had no idea where this was going, if anywhere, but she was smitten, and that was enough to provide her a modicum of joy right now in her difficult life.

To her surprise, Jansen stopped abruptly and turned back to her with a more serious expression, appearing as though he needed to divulge some vital piece of information. The young man got close to Arielle again and spoke in a hushed tone.

"Are you any good at trivia?" he asked.

She entertained the rather random question. "I'm okay, I guess. No serious *Jeopardy* potential, but I've been known to hold my own here on pub trivia nights when I can make it."

"You mentioned needing to make more money, right? My buddy did this experimental, underground trivia thing, like, six months ago. Apparently, you can win half a million if you do well enough," Jansen said.

The young woman was now very curious but tried to downplay her interest. "How much did your friend win?"

"Fifty grand," he answered.

"Did you ever try it?"

He laughed lightly. "I'm not into games."

She smirked and silently contemplated the information.

"Listen, no pressure, but think about it." He retrieved a pen from out of his jacket and then gently took her hand. "If you're interested, this is the address…" He wrote the peculiar URL, across the palm of her hand: *trivialab6g4upl7pt8ludc2m.onion.*

"This looks… bizarre," she said with a chuckle.

"It's a dark web address. I know this all seems weird and shady, but I promise you, it's legit. The company uses the dark web because they don't want a horde of game-show wannabes trying to get in on the action and turn the whole thing into a circus. They rely primarily on word of mouth," he explained.

"And you just remember this long-ass address off the top of your head? Do they pay you to pitch this?" she inquired with a gutsy grin.

"I won't lie to you. My buddy gets a generous commission for referrals. I sort of got in on that, too," he replied. "It's nice pocket money, and I don't have to do anything other than mention this to people who like high-stakes trivia... or people who might really need the cash.”

Arielle then gazed at the URL, still processing. “The dark web isn’t illegal, is it?”

“No, it’s just more private, perfect for stuff like this. But you’ll have to download Tor, though. It’s a browser for the dark web. You can find it on Google,” Jansen instructed. “If you do apply for this, tell them Ronnie’s friend referred you. This could seriously change everything for you and your mom, Arielle. I’m so rooting for you.”

Arielle looked into his caring eyes and saw a glimpse of a brighter future, even amid her uneasiness over the idea of jumping this far out of her comfort zone.

She drove home in silence, weighing the pros and cons of this unique opportunity. Upon her arrival, a fresh pile of bills waiting for her on the kitchen table was all she needed to force a decision.

After making sure her mother was settled in comfortably for the night, Arielle grabbed her laptop and sat on top of her bed, ready to do it. The glow of the screen provided a dim light in her darkened bedroom. She followed Jansen's instructions and downloaded the special web browser – Tor. Then, she typed in that odd URL, which took her to a very basic webpage with a header that read: TRIVIA LAB.

The crude site, like something from the internet circa 1998, was nothing more than a set of simple form fields to enter personal information for the purpose of applying to the contest. Once she typed in her info, she clicked to submit the application form. It was done. Then, she waited.

Three days later, Arielle received an encrypted text stating that she had been accepted to play the game. The company emailed her some preliminary paperwork, which she completed and sent back in a timely manner. She was eager to get in and win some much-needed money to offset the mounting debt. To her surprise, she was informed that the company paid for her to stay in a nice hotel on the outskirts of the city, for the night before she was due to report to play the game. In addition, she was provided round-trip transportation for the entirety of the process, in the form of a company limousine. These unexpected amenities certainly made Arielle feel more relaxed and reassured about her decision to play this game.

As promised, the limousine picked her up at her house at 4 PM on the day before she was to play. About twenty minutes later, she arrived at the elegant Branchmore Hotel, where a special concierge cordially greeted her in the impressive lobby.

"Good afternoon, Ms. Callow. It's an honor to have you here at the Branchmore. I'm happy to inform you that your suite is ready. If there is anything we can provide for you, please don't hesitate to call down to my desk. My name is Pierre, and I'm the special concierge serving our VIP guests."

"Wow, thank you so much. I feel like a celebrity," Arielle said.

Pierre grinned lightly. "That's our goal here, and we are devoted to it. On a side note, I must inform you that I have been instructed by your hosts to procure and hold both your driver's license and cell phone tomorrow morning before you depart for the game. This is their standard protocol, implemented for security purposes and the integrity of the contest. Both items will be returned to you when you return to the hotel following the game."

Arielle was rather confused by the mandate, but she didn't make a fuss about it. She was beginning to grasp and accept the level of secrecy required to take part in this game.

The night came and went, and the big morning arrived. The hotel was a real treat, even though Arielle didn't get much sleep due to her jitters over the imminent experience.

After a light breakfast, she relinquished her driver's license and phone to the special concierge and boarded the limousine to embark on this uncertain adventure.

Before they drove off, the driver instructed Arielle to put on a soft, black blindfold that rested in a compartment in the backseat area, near the middle console. He explained that this was to be worn for the duration of the ride. The young woman obliged, understanding the secretive nature of this project, and wore the blindfold while she sat quietly in the back.

The drive felt long, but it must have been no more than a half hour. Arielle could hear the limousine pull into an underground garage of some sort before the driver announced their arrival and permitted her to remove the blindfold.

After exiting the vehicle, the young woman found herself in the drab confines of a parking garage that was also the lowest-level entry point of what appeared, at first glance, to be an industrial-looking building. Without further delay, two stoic associates appeared and escorted Arielle inside the gloomy location. It was time for the games to begin.

The room was cold and stark, with concrete walls and an imposing metal table at its center. Arielle sat at the table, her expression a mix of eagerness and nervousness. Harnessed to the chair and shackled to the table, she glanced around the drab, Russian-interrogation-style room, taking in the oppressive atmosphere.

The sound of footsteps approaching from the hall broke the silence of the room. Two well-dressed professionals entered: Quizzer Y – a man in his forties, and Quizzer X – a woman in her thirties. Each carried a laptop and a clipboard filled with documents. Arielle also noticed that both of these official individuals seemed to have the same tattoo as Jansen—the spotted, gray and brown bobcat head with golden eyes—tucked in subtly on the underside of their left wrists.

"Good day to you, Ms. Callow," Quizzer Y said, his voice formal but not unfriendly.

Arielle forced a polite yet apprehensive smile. Quizzer X closed the door behind them and locked it before both quizzers took their seats across from her at the table. They set up their laptops and organized the paperwork on their clipboards, engaging in idle chit-chat to ease the tension.

"I do hope your stay with us last evening was satisfactory," Quizzer Y said.

"Yes... certainly. The hotel was... quite lovely," Arielle replied, her voice trembling slightly.

"Good to hear," Quizzer Y said. "A strange bed can often make sleep and comfort rather difficult."

"Especially with this awful weather lately," added Quizzer X. "Hard for anyone to sleep."

Arielle relaxed a bit, grateful for the small talk. "Most definitely. I never cared for the rain. At least, not this much of it. My leaky roof and drafty windows are no strangers to it."

Quizzer Y sighed and looked over one particular document from his clipboard. "Ah, yes. Here we are."

He then slid two documents over to Arielle: a signed affidavit and a release form. "Just a formality, but a necessary one for our legal protection. Can you confirm for us that this is your signature on this affidavit and this release form?"

Arielle studied the documents briefly. "Yes. I remember signing these. Two weeks ago, I believe."

"And you understood their contents and agreed to the binding terms and declarations made within them?" Quizzer Y asked.

Arielle nodded, her anxiety rising once more. "Yes."

"Very good. Then we can continue as planned," Quizzer Y said, putting away the legal documents while Quizzer X pulled up a file on her laptop.

Quizzer Y explained, "As you know, this experiment is being conducted as part of a study through the International College of the Commons. It is merely a quiz game designed to gather social and psychological information that could benefit us all as a society. This session here will be video recorded in its entirety. Our apologies for the restraints securing you in place. I realize they must seem intimidating and highly unusual, but positional stability is an important part of this study."

"And we do thank you for joining this study," Quizzer X added.

"I don't mean to be rude, but about the prize..." Arielle inquired timidly.

"Ah, right. The prize," Quizzer Y responded. "Should you make it to the end of each round, you will be awarded an increasing fee—or prize—as laid out in the agreement you signed."

"Thank you," Arielle said. "It would mean so much to me to..."

Snapping into a more aggressive demeanor, Quizzer Y sharply interrupted Arielle as his partner handed him a quiz sheet from her clipboard papers. "Right, moving along then. Question 1: What is the capital city of France?"

Arielle hesitated, expecting a more challenging question. "Paris?"

"Correct," Quizzer Y replied. "Question 1A: In what year did the Estates General ignite the French Revolution?"

The question left Arielle momentarily speechless. "Pardon me?"

"Ten seconds. I'll need an answer," Quizzer Y demanded.

"Uh... 1850?" Arielle guessed.

Without delay, Quizzer X produced a small baton from her blazer and pressed it against Arielle's shackled arm. A jolt of electricity surged through the young woman, causing her to jerk in her seat.

"Oh, my God! What was that?!" Arielle cried out, her face contorted in shock and pain.

The quizzers' demeanor turned cold and businesslike. "I'm afraid the correct answer is 1789. Moving on..." Quizzer Y said, his tone devoid of sympathy. "Question 2: How many sides does a triangle contain?"

Still reeling from the shock, Arielle took a moment before answering, "Uh, three. Three, of course."

"Correct," Quizzer Y replied. "Question 2A: As is based on the Euclidean geometry of right triangles, recite the equational form of the Pythagorean theorem."

"I have no idea what you just said. Triangle equations? I was always terrible with math," Arielle said.

"We'll need an answer, please," Quizzer X said.

"Ten seconds," Quizzer Y added.

Arielle struggled to think, but time quickly ran out.

"I'm afraid the time has expired," Quizzer Y stated.

Arielle attempted to voice her frustration. "These questions seem too..."

Before Arielle could fully express her discontent, Quizzer X used the baton again, this time, increasing the voltage and pressing the device firmly into the young woman's ribs. The jolt caused Arielle to convulse violently. After a moment, Quizzer X withdrew the baton.

"Next question..." Quizzer Y said.

Arielle struggled to recover from the severe shock. "Please... I can't do this anymore."

Quizzer X stood up and walked toward the door as Quizzer Y nonchalantly read the next question.

"Question 3: Which internal organ is responsible for circulating blood through the human body?"

While Quizzer X briefly stepped out of the room, Arielle pleaded. "The heart. Please stop. I want to go home."

"Correct," Quizzer Y responded.

Quizzer X re-entered, closing the door tightly behind her as she carried in a medium-sized metal box, which she soon set down on the table in front of Arielle before taking her seat once again. Arielle's eyes widened with horror at the sound of strange rustling coming from within the mysterious box.

"What is that? What's in there?" she asked.

"Within the four equal compartments of this box, there are two snakes, ten spiders, forty cockroaches, and three Asian centipedes, respectively," Quizzer X explained.

The fear on Arielle's face was palpable.

"Question 3A: Who invented the first patented artificial heart for human use?" Quizzer Y asked.

Without hesitation, Arielle exclaimed, "Paul Winchell! Paul Winchell!"

Quizzer Y nodded with a slight air of disappointment. "Correct. It appears your nursing career came in quite handy for answering those last two questions."

Arielle breathed a sigh of relief as Quizzer Y gestured to his partner. Quizzer X then took back the metal box and exited the room.

"Moving on to the second-to-last question of the round. Who wrote the iconic children's book *The Cat in the Hat*?" Quizzer Y asked.

Arielle, exhausted and battered, remained mentally alert for her survival. "Dr. Seuss."

Quizzer X re-entered the room and took her seat once more.

Quizzer Y responded to Arielle. "That is correct. Question 4A: What are the surnames of the five Russian families characterized in Leo Tolstoy's epic novel *War and Peace*?"

Feeling the weight of impending defeat, Arielle lowered her head.

"Ten seconds," Quizzer Y announced.

Summoning her last reserves of strength, Arielle raised her head again and defiantly met Quizzer Y's gaze. "Fuck you."

Quizzer Y responded with an indifferent formality. "Incorrect, I'm afraid."

He turned to his partner and gave another nod of the head. Quizzer X rose from her seat and whipped out her baton once more, immediately striking Arielle across the head with the weapon. The brutal impact knocked the young woman out cold.

Arielle awakened groggily, her senses slowly returning. She found herself in the same room, still shackled to the table and chair. There was no way for her to gauge the amount of time she was unconscious or what had happened during that period. An eerie, orange light now lit the room dimly, and the quizzers were nowhere to be found.

Suddenly, heavy slamming and primal growling emanated from the other side of the door. Blood-thirsty snarls accompanied the hostile sounds of someone—or something—trying to break into the room. Panic-stricken, Arielle struggled to free herself from her restraints.

"Help! Help me! Let me out!"

Amid the chaos, Quizzer Y's voice cut through over built-in speakers hidden somewhere in the room. "Ms.

Callow. We'll need an answer to the final question of the round."

"Please, let me out! Let me out of here!" Arielle screamed.

The pounding on the door intensified, and the growls turned louder and more menacing.

Quizzer Y's voice cut through again, calm and detached, as always. "The answer, please. Ten seconds remain before the door opens."

"I don't know the question!" Arielle shrieked. "I don't know the fucking question!"

The young woman's cries bounced off the faded concrete walls of this disturbing space. Her time was up.

To her absolute terror, a buzzer sounded sharply, and the door automatically unlocked. Without a second's delay, it burst open completely, and the stuff of pure nightmares emerged from the darkness on the other side.

It was the bobcat creature that must have inspired the notorious wrist tattoo—a mega-beast bearing grayish-brown fur with black spots and stripes—a coat accented by piercing, golden eyes that almost glowed. Blood and saliva dripped from its long, sharp fangs. It was easily three times the size of a normal, fully grown adult bobcat in the wild. This monster had to be a genetic lab concoction, and it wasted no time charging at its fresh, new prey.

Arielle screamed and toppled over backward in her chair, taking the table down with her, turning it into shield of sorts. The vicious creature chomped at the young woman but couldn't get to her as the table blocked out the relentless attack. The beast snarled and chewed violently at the table, however, each bite potentially getting it closer to Arielle's tender flesh and crunchy bones.

The young woman screeched in fear, making the beast even more eager to get to her. Realizing that there wasn't much table left to protect her, Arielle made the bold decision to simultaneously kick and push the table forcefully in an upward motion to try and knock the bobcat away. The move worked, ramming the creature aside and also breaking the now-compromised restraints that had Arielle locked to the furniture.

She jumped up to her feet and made a beeline for the door before the ferocious bobcat could recover and pursue her again. Emerging into a dim, industrial-looking hallway made entirely of concrete, Arielle found herself facing the barrels of two AR-15s brandished by a pair of private military guards, both male, wearing gray battle camo uniforms.

"Hold it right there! Don't fucking move!" one of the guards shouted.

Arielle froze and stared defiantly into the man's eyes. Before he could issue her another command, the bobcat charged out of the room and lunged at the two guards, who happened to be closer to the demolished doorway than the escaped young woman. Unable to fire off any shots to strike the beast, the men were torn apart in less than thirty seconds.

Arielle seized the moment and sprinted away down the hall, taking refuge in the first unlocked room she could find.

Her getaway landed her in a small control room with a table that hosted three computers and at least six monitors displaying camera views of several rooms and hallways in this bunker-like complex of depravity.

Arielle's eyes soon caught two figures on one of the monitors. They hurried down the same hallway she just navigated moments ago, eventually stopping outside of this control room. Arielle leaned in closer to the monitor, for a better look.

These panicking, desperate figures were the two quizzers that put Arielle in this dangerous situation. Now, they were the victims, pounding fearfully on the locked control room door and begging for entry. Arielle thought about it for a moment, deliberating mercy. She then straightened up, crossed her arms defiantly, and did nothing.

Her eyes locked onto the monitor to watch as the bobcat raced in for another set of kills directly outside the door to this room. The quizzers had no chance. They were mauled and devoured even swifter than the guards. The rogue bobcat was eating well and was definitely not ready to call it a day.

Arielle saw that the beast was still outside the door, sniffing intensely. It could detect familiar flesh inside the room. Realizing that she was stuck again, she quietly backed herself up into the corner, where her heel bumped an open box of DVD-R discs. The sudden noise seized the instant attention of the creature, which let out a low, guttural growl directly at the door.

Arielle's curiosity got the better of her, and she knelt down to have a look at the contents of the box. Inside, there were dozens and dozens of discs in cases, each case marked with a first name, a date, and a price—the cheapest at five hundred bucks. With trembling hands, she whipped out one of the discs and popped it into a nearby computer's disc desk.

The video loaded and played on one of the monitors, showing another person strapped to the table and chair in the quizzing room. This person, a young man, was also unable to answer successfully, but unlike Arielle's feat, he could not escape the wrath of the bobcat. The recording captured every grisly moment of the kill, forcing Arielle to slam the buttons on the disc deck in order to stop the video from playing any further. It was all too clear now that this operation was not what it seemed.

The slamming started again. The bobcat attacked this door as it did to the quizzing-room door not long ago. Arielle flinched with terror at every hit and scratch the beast delivered to try and gain access to her. Desperately, the young woman scanned the space with her eyes, looking for any way out of there.

She stepped forward and tripped over the box of discs, moving it aside about a foot or so, which exposed an inconspicuous hatch in the floor. Yanking on its handle proved futile at first; it wouldn't budge. The bobcat was making headway at the door, savagely smashing and tearing open two sizable chunks of it while growling and snarling with primal aggression.

Arielle frantically worked on the handle, loosening it up a bit with each distraught tug and pull. The holes torn open in the door gave way enough for the creature to reach into the room and swat its sharp claws as it continued forcing its way through the weakening barrier. It could smell the next course of its extended meal, and there wasn't much time before it gained access to it.

Holding nothing back, Arielle yanked on the handle forcefully until it finally popped loose. At the same time, the door to the room crashed apart, and the bobcat began making a full entry. Arielle flipped open the hatch and peered down at what looked to be an aluminum slide of some kind—a clandestine escape route for the members of this twisted organization. There was no time to waste. She jumped down into the hatch and slid to an uncertain destination just as the bobcat positioned itself to make a fatal pounce.

Shadows flashed by Arielle as she flew speedily down the steep, enclosed slide, narrowly evading death by beast moments before. Her mind raced with a new panic, realizing death could also await her at the other end of this slide, but it was a chance she had to take. Finally, the dark enclosure opened up, and the slide ended.

Momentum tossed her out of the mysterious building, via a trap door in a brick wall, and into a pile of dirt and light junk on the cool, damp blacktop of a quiet alleyway. She wished that she could have stolen a few minutes to recover from the drop, but she knew she couldn't hang around and risk facing any further life-threatening danger.

The young woman picked herself up and jogged out of the alley, landing in a desolate, abandoned industrial section of an urban locale. This dilapidated area intimidated her almost as much as the inside of the ominous building she just escaped, so she kept running until she found something familiar that could aid her in getting her bearings.

After almost three exhausting miles of urgent running, a familiar landmark came in the form of the last station on the train route she normally took to work every morning. Arielle never had a need to come out this far on the train, and the young woman knew that this point was the final stop on the route, even though she hadn't seen it in person before this moment. Now, it was essential for her to board at this stop. Of course, her public transit card was at home, so she feverishly scoured the street surfaces in front of her and somehow managed to rustle up barely enough discarded change to get a ticket to ride.

An array of strong and varying emotions pulsed through Arielle while she sat on the moving train and gazed out the window—exhaustion, rage, confusion, depression, uncertainty, disappointment, fear. She felt like a dumb, desperate idiot to fall into something like this, but her dire need for financial support seemed to cloud her better judgment. Thoughts of her mother then passed through her mind, and the tears just poured from her eyes.

Arielle got off the train at her usual station and walked home on foot, arriving close to sundown. She slipped into the house softly, with few words, to avoid her mother and the visiting aide seeing her battered condition. The young woman grabbed a fast shower and changed into jeans and a dark hoodie before she used the landline phone in her mom's room to quietly call her best friend, who answered after a few rings.

"Hello?"

"Em? It's me," Arielle replied in a serious tone.

"Hey, Arielle. Sorry I didn't answer right away. I didn't recognize the number," Emma said, trying to talk over a lot of noise in the background.

"I'm calling from our landline," Arielle explained. "Where are you?"

"At the tavern. Wait, are you home now? How did everything go? Did you win? Oh, my God! Tell me everything! No, actually, I'll come over right now!" Emma said.

"Is he there?" Arielle questioned.

"Who?"

"Mr. Wonderful..."

Emma peered around the tavern and observed Jansen at the bar, with his friends, just like before. She told Arielle, "Yeah, he's here, drinking with his buddies. Hey, have you been going out with him? You two would seriously make a really cute couple..."

Arielle interrupted her. "Emma, do me a favor. Go home and lock your doors. If Rosy and Greg are with you, tell them to do the same thing."

"Uh, you're kind of scaring me here, Arielle. What the hell is going on?"

"I'll tell you later. But first, I have to go to the hospital and pick up a few things," Arielle replied before ending the call abruptly.

Emma, Rosy, and Greg followed Arielle's orders and had gone straight home over an hour earlier. Jansen had shifted away from his own friends and moved to a booth, where he sat with a young lady he met earlier in the evening. The two enjoyed some drinks and conversed casually.

"Wow, a teacher and a volunteer helping the homeless. You're my new hero," he said.

The young woman blushed. "I love what I do. I love being a teacher. I wish they'd pay us more, though.

My salary ain't cutting it, and I still owe forty grand in student loans."

"I hear you. You deserve better. I'm impressed that those hardships didn't jade your spirit. Most people in your shoes would turn bad or go crazy. You're an incredible, inspiring woman. I hope you see that when you look in the mirror," he said.

"You are too sweet," she replied, smitten with his charm.

"Hey, maybe there's a way... Eh, you probably wouldn't be interested..." he began.

She perked up with curiosity. "No, what were you going to say?"

"What if I knew a pretty solid way to maybe put a few extra bucks in your pocket?"

"If it's dealing coke, I'll have to give up the whole elementary-school teacher thing. The people in charge typically aren't very keen on drug lords working around the kids," she said with a chuckle.

He grinned and nodded. "Nah, nothing that exciting, unfortunately. But maybe something a teacher could do really well with."

"I'm listening," she said.

"Hey, could you excuse me for a sec? I need to use the restroom. When I come back, I'll fill you in on it. For real, though. A smart teacher like you? You could make some serious bank."

The young woman seemed genuinely intrigued at this potential opportunity to shed some of her mounting debt. Jansen had her full attention and was ready to pitch to her once he returned from the men's room.

He stepped into the restroom and made sure no one else was in there before he took out his cell phone and checked his texts. He had texted one particular number over ten times in the last few hours, but there were no replies. Frustrated, he dialed the number. It rang twice and then went straight to voicemail.

He left a terse message. "Hey, it's me. I've texted you, like, a dozen times tonight. What the hell is going on? I've got two more fish. I'm reeling in the second one right now. I need you to text me ASAP."

After ending the call, he marched over to the urinals, which were positioned in the far corner of the room, obscured by a row of about five stalls. He unzipped and relieved himself at the urinal closest to the end stall.

The quiet was soon broken by what sounded like the restroom door creaking open from across the room. However, the noise was so swift and soft that the young man couldn't be sure. He continued doing his business peacefully until another subtle noise grabbed his sharp attention. This time, it was some light, intermittent clicking and shuffling in the stalls. Jansen held still and listened closely, unsure of what he was hearing.

"Hello?... Anyone in here?"

The noises instantly ceased, and there was no response to his uneasy question. A peculiar tension then fell over the room. Suddenly, Jansen felt a surge of excruciating, ungodly pain in the back of his ankle. He peered down and observed blood pouring out of his Achilles tendon, which had just been severed with quick precision.

He let out a yelp and stumbled backward in shock. The door to the stall closest to him burst open, and a stealthy figure emerged determinedly. It was Arielle, dressed in her jeans and dark hoodie, with the hood pulled up. A plastic bobcat mask covered her face, and she wore latex medical gloves on her hands. Blood dripped from the razor-sharp scalpel she gripped tightly. The surgical tool had an elongated triangular blade with a hypotenuse edge, and Jansen's tendon got a surprise introduction to every millimeter of it.

She pounced on top of the writhing young man and slashed him again with the surgical instrument, this time across the chest and on his flailing hands and arms.

"No, please! I'm sorry!" he shouted.

Arielle whipped out a Hoke osteotome—a sharp blade for cutting bone. Jansen attempted to sit up, and the young woman responded with a strike to his face. The tool cut across his orbital area and sliced open his right eye. Blood and ocular fluid spurted out and then gushed down his cheek and neck. He screeched in pain, and his adrenaline took over.

The villain forcefully shoved Arielle off of him and managed to pull himself up to a wobbly standing position. The young woman reached out with the osteotome, aiming it under Jansen's buttocks. In one swift slicing motion, she gashed open his scrotum and perineum. Blood and fluid splashed out onto the floor and poured down his legs before he collapsed like a ton of bricks, unconscious from the brutal attack.

Without batting an eye, Arielle sneaked out of the place as slyly as she slipped in. She left a simple hand-written note on the door of the restroom: *Better call 911. There's a bad boy in here.* About five minutes later, an unlucky patron found the note and the shocking, gory scene inside the restroom. The police and para-medics arrived soon thereafter to cart Jansen off to the hospital, where he barely survived his grisly injuries.

Arielle went to the police and disclosed her terror at the hands of Jansen and his maniacal cohorts with the sadistic snuff-video syndicate. The scandalous story rocked the nation and beyond. Arielle and her mother never had to worry about money again after the book deals and interview offers came rolling in.

Following his violent restroom assault and grueling recovery, Jansen was arrested, tried, and sentenced to life in prison. The authorities, however, never caught his restroom attacker. The few surviving members of the syndicate were ultimately apprehended and sentenced to long, hard prison terms. The staggering horrors of what transpired through this heinous conspiracy lingered hauntingly within the country's psyche that year, like Helter Skelter, Jonestown, and Columbine did in their respective eras.

The bobcat disappeared after Arielle thwarted the diabolical operations at the building in the city. Experts believe the formidable beast broke out of the comprised structure after its fierce yet unsuccessful pursuit of the tenacious young woman. Somewhere, though, it lies and waits, stalking its next kill and lurking in the shadows of the streets and the dark fog of our nightmares.

THE END

Studying under esteemed writers Sonny Sykes and Charles McClelland, Bill Freas continued his education at West Chester University before he was hired in 2002 as the head writer of a TBS sketch-comedy pilot that ultimately did not make it to series. Subsequently, he optioned or sold over two dozen scripts, which included shorts, features, and pilots. As an author, he has written more than twenty published short stories, including three full collections. His produced credits as a writer span multiple genres and mediums. Currently, Bill also heads up Oceanicom Films' development department, where he oversees the development of US and international film and TV projects for the Australian company. Along with script, development, and production consultation, Bill is also a staff writer for Vancouver production company Foresight Entertainment, with which he has had an active partnership for over fifteen years.

Chapter 6
Deadly Bytes

Ian Gielen

Detective Dave Calahan sat back in his chair, wearing a satisfied smile, after making the final adjustment to his horrifying animatronic bugbear. After a few moments of rest, he rose to his feet and double-checked his work, ensuring everything was in place before closing the panel on the back of the imposing six-foot monster. Grabbing a USB cable from the bench, he inserted it into the hidden slot beneath the panel, then connected it to the USB port on his computer. Now, all that remained was to test all its features, and he could finally call it a night.

Dave, an enthusiastic lover of horror and fantasy, had been designing and constructing animatronic creatures since his early twenties, even before he ventured into a career in law enforcement. Despite having less free time nowadays, he still managed to complete a few of the monstrosities each month. It was an expensive hobby, but he loved it, and there was nothing like bringing a creature from his worst nightmares to life. He even sold some of them to his friends and acquaintances when Halloween rolled around.

The bugbear, a terrifying amalgamation of demon and bear, all fur, teeth and claws, would stay with him in his horror room, adding to the collection of terrifying creatures. The werewolf, giant spider, zombie, and demon were already there, each capable of realistic movements and eerie sound effects.

Sitting down at the computer, he tapped a few keys to bring up his simple but effective custom-made control software and tapped on the button to raise the creature's arm. With a mechanical whir, the bugbear's arm extended obediently upwards. He pressed the button to bring it down, and the creature's arm swung down smoothly and rested at its side. He systematically clicked on each button, testing every function of the creature until he was satisfied. With a yawn, he settled into his chair and glanced at his watch, only to be startled by the glowing green clock face, which read 11:12 pm.

"Shit," he muttered under his breath, hastily rolling his chair back and springing to his feet. With a 5:30 am wake-up call looming, he knew the exhaustion of starting the work week with little sleep would be hard to shake.

Just as he was heading towards his bedroom, his work phone started buzzing in his pocket. He let out a frustrated sigh. It seemed like he wouldn't get any rest tonight.

Retrieving his phone from his pocket, he accepted the call, already bracing himself for a long night ahead.

The moment he noticed the officer's expression of shock on his pale face at the entrance of the run-down apartment building as he pulled up, he realized that what awaited him would be anything but pleasant. The dilapidated building exuded an air of neglect and decay, with peeling paint and broken windows. After nodding to the officer at the door, he stepped into the hallway and was met with an overpowering stench, forcing him to quickly pinch his nose.

The floor was a mess, with rubbish scattered everywhere. Rare glimpses of the floor through the rubbish revealed decaying floorboards underneath. The walls were stained yellow and peeling, revealing the layers beneath. The stairs directly in front of him were flanked by a rusting metal guardrail, with several sections missing.

In the small space behind the stairs, discarded bags of trash had been left to rot as flies buzzed lazily around them. Dave's face twisted in disgust, feeling his stomach churn and his gorge rise. He could deal with the horror of almost any crime scene, but it turns out that the smell of decaying garbage was his Achilles heel.

Keeping his nose pinched, Dave made his way up to the second floor and down a narrow hallway to apartment 223. Ducking under the police tape, he ran into the photographer Mark, who had just wrapped up and was heading to the door. His face was as pale as the police officer's guarding the entrance downstairs.

"Hey Mark, what have we got?"

"A big damn mess, that's what," Mark said with a grimace. "In all my years of photographing horrific crime scenes, this one is pretty high up there."

He paused, a visible shudder running down his body.

"Now, if you'll excuse me, I have to get these processed and then wash my eyes out with bleach. See you at the station later?"

Dave nodded and pressed himself against the wall as Mark, clearly shaken, hurried past him towards the exit, eager to leave.

Dave shrugged and pressed forward, only to come to an abrupt stop as he turned the corner, his eyes widening at the sight of the horrifying scene that greeted him.

The living room stretched out in front of him, a nightmarish scene of carnage. Blood stained every inch, with bits of flesh and body organs clinging to the walls, ceiling, sofa, TV, and its stand. Next to the overturned sofa, the remnants of the victim's body lay in a gruesome heap. Scattered across the room were numerous drones of varying sizes, from palm-sized to over a meter long, some broken while others remained whole, but all with blades stained with blood.

"Looks like the damn drones came to life and attacked the poor bastard."

Sam, the medical examiner, rose to his feet from his position near a numbered tag where a blood-coated drone lay overturned.

"It certainly looks that way," Dave remarked, taking in the sight of the number tags, the bloody drones, and the deep, jagged cuts on what remained of the body.

"The wounds match the blades perfectly. There are no other marks on the body that would indicate other weapons were used, but an autopsy will confirm that. There are no signs of forced entry. The doors and windows were all still locked from the inside."

"So, either the guy was terrible at controlling his drones, or someone else was controlling them remotely."

"Seems that way," Sam nodded in agreement.

"Wait, what's that?" Dave asked, his attention drawn to a blinking red light on an otherwise dark computer monitor in the corner.

"Don't know, but I'll leave you to it. I'll organize forensics and transport for the body."

Dave waved in response as he stepped around the bloodstains and viscera to get to the workstation. In stark contrast to the rest of the building and the old and worn contents in this apartment, the PC under the desk appeared to be state-of-the-art. The monitor on the desk was small but seemed to be similarly high-tech.

Now that he was closer to it, he could see the screen was flashing with the same red words appearing at regular intervals on an otherwise black screen.

Connect Phone to USB to unlock

Pulling on some rubber gloves he had stuffed into his pockets, he tapped on the keyboard, hoping that it was just a screensaver, but there was no response.

With a curious frown, he bent down to examine the PC below the desk. As he suspected, he found a USB cable plugged into the front slot of the PC, which had fallen onto the floor during the attack. Lifting it up, he saw the flat, rectangular head of a USB-C connector. Standing back up, he scanned the room, his eyes landing on the victim's phone a few meters away. Its screen was shattered, and deep cuts marked the casing, mirroring the injuries on the body.

Sighing in frustration, Dave fished out his work phone from his pocket. Luckily, his department was not stingy in its funding, so he had the latest iPhone, which would fit the cable, but he knew plugging it in would be a bad idea. He should call in the tech guys to handle it.

He glanced at his watch: 4:25 am. Jack, his boss, was always on his ass about getting his cases wrapped up faster, and he was already way behind in his paperwork. If he found something now, it might keep him off his back, at least for a day or two. Besides, it wasn't as if it was his personal phone. If something happened to his work phone, he could easily get it replaced.

Shrugging, he set his phone on the table and plugged in the cable. In response, the monitor flickered to life, displaying a mesmerizing, multicolored loading icon for a moment before revealing a web browser logged into a website. It only took a few seconds for him to realise this wasn't any regular browser. It was the Tor browser, known for its use in navigating the Dark Web. A mere few clicks unveiled the use of a VPN, and a simple glance at the browser's address confirmed the inclusion of the .onion domain.

"What do we have here? Looks like someone's been a naughty boy."

Without interacting with anything on the site, Dave scrolled down the page, taking in the content as he went. The website seemed to be a digital landfill, housing an assortment of illegal programs. From what Dave could see, there was a mixture of viruses listed, ranging from those stealthily collecting user information to ones capable of causing irreversible damage to infected systems. There was also an abundance of hacking programs designed to exploit various systems and programs.

The account's log revealed that the last activity had been the personal upload of an AI program devoid of any accompanying details as to what its purpose was. Just as he was about to click on the entry, the monitor went dark.

"Damn it," Dave muttered while crouching down to inspect the PC. It had been shut down. Pressing the power button did nothing. Despite meticulously inspecting all the cables and plugs and attempting another restart, the computer remained unresponsive.

"Just my luck," Dave said with a heavy sigh of frustration.

He checked his watch again, 4:52 a.m. If he arranged the Digital Forensics Team and got the M.E. and CSI team to contact him when they were done, then he could maybe grab a few hours of sleep before he had to go into the office.

Dialing the first of his calls as he walked back to the car, he exited the building and nodded at the still-pale face of the police officer at the entrance. He was in his car, finishing up his last call to CSI, when the sharp insistent beep of a message on his personal phone drew his attention.

"Now what?" he said, his voice tinged with growing frustration. All he wanted to do was crawl into bed and squeeze in what little rest he could.

Removing the phone from the glove box, he took a quick glance at the screen. The message was from an unfamiliar number, and it simply said,

Hello

Must be a wrong number, he thought. Without a second thought, he tucked it into his pocket and set off on his way back home.

It took him thirty minutes to get there, and by the time he reached his front door, he could barely keep his eyes open. He dragged himself down the hallway towards his bedroom, only to be startled by the beeping of his phone.

Pulling it out of his pocket, he glanced at the screen and did a double take. On his way home, two messages had been sent to him, both of which had gone unnoticed.

Both messages came from the same unfamiliar number as the first one. Two of them repeated the initial message, *Hello*. The one he had just received said, *Hello Dave*.

He paused in front of his bedroom door, gazing at it longingly before quickly typing out a response.

Who is this?

Three dots appeared instantly, hovering on the screen a moment before the reply came through.

Do you like monsters, Dave?

An icy chill shot down Dave's spine as he read the words. Sure, he'd told many of his friends and workmates about his hobby, but he had all of their numbers stored on his phone. This was from a new number. He supposed it could have been possible that one of them had bought a brand new phone with a different number.

He tapped out a response.

Whoever this is, it will need to wait. I've just come back from a crime scene and am about to grab a few hours sleep. Talk later.

He pocketed the phone and made a beeline for the bathroom to relieve himself. He was about to head to bed, exhausted and ready to collapse, when the message tone rang out again, breaking the silence. His anger rising, he yanked his phone out of his pocket and stared at the message in shock.

You mean the one in apartment 223? I was there too.

Dave thought back to who he'd seen at the crime scene. There were only the three he'd met, the officer who he'd seen around the precinct a few times, Mark, the photographer, and Sam, the M.E. both of which he'd worked alongside for a few years now. Could it be that the murderer sent the messages?

He typed out another reply.

Is this Mark or Sam? Or are you the police officer I met before I went in?

Three dots immediately danced on the screen, yet no reply followed. Dave stood there for several minutes, staring at the phone screen expectantly, but there was no response.

"Screw this," he muttered to himself before he switched the phone off. Whoever it was could wait. Once he found out who was responsible, there would be hell to pay.

As soon as he collapsed into bed, exhaustion overtook him and he drifted off, but his slumber was short-lived as the shrill ring of the landline phone shattered the silence, startling him awake.

It rang again before he picked it up, expecting it to be related to the new case.

"Hello, Dave. Do you like monsters?"

Despite the obvious intention to frighten him, the cold, robotic, and monotone voice on the other end of the phone only sparked his anger, making his muscles stiffen and his veins pulsate with a burning rage.

"Listen, whoever this is, I'm going to kick your ass. I don't care who you are. When I find you, I'll make you sorry you were born. Now fuck off and leave me alone."

In a fit of rage, he slammed the handset down and ripped out the coiled cord that snaked from the back of the landline phone. Another thing he would have to deal with tomorrow—a landline phone replacement. He reached toward his work phone lying next to it and hesitated. He really should keep it on in case he got a legitimate call, but he was exhausted. Deciding to risk it, he turned it off before settling back down into bed, drifting off almost immediately into unconsciousness.

"Hello, Dave."

Every room in his house seemed to reverberate with the cold, robotic words, as if they were emanating from every electronic device within, incessantly repeating, beating against his skull. Dave covered his ears with his hands, trying to keep the deafening roar of the words at bay, but to no avail.

In a fit of rage, Dave ripped out anything plugged into the wall and hurled any battery-operated devices he could find onto the floor, but it was no use. The words seemed to scream from the very walls them-selves, slipping through the gaps between his fingers that were clasped over his ears, almost as if they were desperate to be heard. Dave tried to drown out the sound with his screams, but it proved futile. Nothing helped.

The volume increased and blood began to pour from his ears. It grew louder still, the relentless sound drilling into his mind and pounding against the walls of his skull. Blood poured out from his ears, his nose, and then his pores, building up immense pressure until his head detonated like a melon, leaving behind a cloud of pink mist.

Dave jolted awake, with his heart pounding and a scream on his lips. His body dripped with sweat, saturating the bedsheets beneath him. He reached for the glass of water on his nightstand and downed it in one go.

"Hello Dave, I like your monsters."

Dave froze, with the glass still pressed to his lips. He slowly lowered the glass and placed it back on the nightstand before turning his head towards the foot of the bed, where an imposing shadow loomed motionless.

"Wh... who are you?"

"I'm your bugbear, Dave. Don't you recognise me?"

The sound of the monotone, robotic voice sent shivers down his spine, but he mustered the courage to reach out and switch on the lamp. The blinding glare of the light overwhelmed Dave's groggy eyes. He shielded his eyes with his hand and strained to see the end of the bed.

Sure enough, it was the bugbear. It stood there, stock still and silent, its artificial eyes seeming to stare directly at him.

"Who are you?" Dave repeated, scooting backwards against the headboard of his bed. "What do you want?"

The creature stood there, its silence filling the air with an eerie stillness. Suddenly, it lunged at him, its massive paws raised, the lamplight reflecting off the sharp, metallic claws Dave had painstakingly designed.

"You, Dave. I want you."

In a desperate attempt, Dave reached for the drawer, only to feel his arm go limp at the creature's assault. Its metallic claws dug deep into his shoulder, mercilessly rending his flesh and leaving it hanging by a few tenuous threads. Blood coated the floor and walls from Dave's ruined shoulder as he writhed in pain.

The sudden trauma left him paralyzed, his body unable to move as the creature pressed its attack, its claws tearing into him, blood and gore sent flying with each strike.

His last vision was of the giant spider, demon, werewolf and zombie animatronic creatures trudging toward the bedroom to join in the slaughter before he fell into the infinite dark. By the time they were done, all that remained of his body was a heap of steaming organs on the bed. The creatures surrounded it in silence, their forms stilled once more, their limbs stained with crimson.

Clay raised his hands towards the ceiling, feeling the stretch in his muscles and following it up with a couple of neck stretches. The wheels of his chair squeaked in protest as he pushed it away from the desk, rising to his feet and embarking on a lap around the Digital Forensics Lab to relieve the stiffness in his legs.

He had been studying the algorithm of the AI program uploaded to the dark web by the victim Nathan Roberts for hours, unravelling its complex logic, waving farewell to his colleagues as they left one by one until he was the only one left in the lab. The victim had programmed it to discover the weakness of any system it was uploaded to and exploit it for the purpose of the uploader. It had the potential to be used for any number of things: blackmail, intimidation, stealing information, impersonation, and even murder.

Nathan had made one crucial error with its development, however. He had made it so intelligent that it had started modifying its own programming as it learned. It had grown almost a will of its own and had developed its own defense mechanisms. It knew Nathan had the ability to terminate it and so it made sure he didn't have the chance to, taking control of his collection of drones to lethal effect.

Once detective Dave Calahan came into the picture, it knew he was the next biggest threat and so he used his hobby, the animatronic creatures, against him.

Fortunately, Clay's weightlifting hobby was not something that could be exploited as a vulnerability.

Still, he needed to be careful. The AI had adapted in ways that Clay hadn't been able to get a handle on just yet. He had put safeguards in place, which would be enough to protect him, but one slip-up could spell disaster.

The phone in his pocket started vibrating. Likely a message from his wife asking him when he was coming home. He was already late by a few hours.

His phone vibrated again. Then again. Then it was nonstop as messages continually flooded his phone.

"What the hell?"

Clay pulled out his phone, his fingers trembling as he scrolled through the messages, his face growing paler as he read each one.

His wife:

What the hell, Clay? My sister? Really? Don't bother coming home.

His boss:

I don't know what the hell possessed you to send pictures like that, but you and I are going to have a little chat tomorrow morning.

His mother:

Clay, I'm so disappointed in you. How could you do something so cruel?

"No... No, no no no no..."

Clay's face glistened with sweat as he logged back into his computer. The AI had somehow bypassed his security wall. It had infiltrated every aspect of his digital life, from his email to his phone and bank account. Not only was it sending messages to his contacts, but it was also using personal and compromising photos he had taken to make each message more targeted and malicious. His life was effectively ruined.

Stunned, Clay sat motionless as the screen before him went dark, leaving only two words in its center.

Hello Clay

Rian Burnhouse is a lifelong fan of fantasy novels, which has translated into a love for writing his own fantasy works and creating Dungeons & Dragons content for his quickly growing YouTube channel. He is currently writing his first novel while growing his fan base as "Dad the Dungeon Master" on YouTube. He spends his free time enjoying his family, writing short stories, and running tabletop games for his friends and YT followers.

Chapter 7
Shadows of the Dark Web
Brad Thomas

Jonathan had been a loner all his life. He flourished in the seclusion of his one-bedroom apartment in the middle of Manhattan, where skyscrapers loomed large, and cast a constant somber shadow across the city.

He worked as a computer programmer during the day, a job that he loved, and at night he observed the shadowy online sites where most people were afraid to venture. His fascination with the forbidden pulled him further into the dark realms of cyberspace, particularly the deep dark web, where unknown dangers and whispered secrets awaited all who dared to enter.

Jonathan always worked hard during his time at work. It was a very rewarding job, and he was hoping to get a promotion very soon. One evening, after a long, tiring shift at work, he returned home. His plan was to shower, eat and relax while having a night off from web browsing... that didn't happen. He threw his bag on the sofa and tossed his keys onto the small wooden coffee table that sat in the center of his living room.

Jonathan sat down at his computer desk; his thin, gaunt face lit up by the brightness of his monitor. He was like a recluse when it came to nighttime; he never went out to see friends, never went on dates, no social-ization of any kind. He preferred his own company.

To be honest, his only friends were online, but they weren't really friends, more like fellow members of a cult or a following. He had come into The Dark Abyss, a disturbing community notorious for its weird and unsettling dark content. It was a well-hidden area of the dark web that not many people knew existed, where users sold and purchased everything from illegal drugs to disturbing videos, each post laced with an air of unsettling content.

Jonathan felt an ice-cold chill run down his spine as he scrolled through the threads, but it was intoxicating and addictive. This was where the real world met the surreal, a place with no consequences where evil thrived.

As the hours passed by, one thread caught his attention: a post titled "Unleash the Shadows." The user, Hugh. R. Doomed, claimed to have discovered something eerie but remarkable, an experimental digital entity that could exist in real life under certain conditions. Jonathan's curiosity got the better of him as he began to read through the thread, absorbing every detail. Messing around with artificial intelligence was his bread and butter, and the idea of blending digital and reality intrigued him.

The thread explained how to access the program, instructing users to download the file and run it while in specific conditions... during a sunset while connected to a dark website known only as "The Forever." Jonathan felt the familiar tug of excitement. This was his chance to push the boundaries of his understanding, to merge technology with what lay hidden in the shadows.

Why do I have to do this at sunset, though? He thought before shrugging it off.

He waited for the sun to set, his heart racing with buzzing anticipation. The sun had finally set as darkness arrived, then he followed the instructions. Carefully, he hit download on the file, ensuring he was connected to The Forever. His screen began flashing a violent hue of crimson as the software installed.

Strips and lines of code danced and flashed before his eyes on the monitor, and he felt the air grow heavy, thickening with an unknown presence. At first, nothing happened. His monitor was flickering softly. As Jonathan leaned closer, the program on the screen began to morph, with shapes appearing in the code that flashed across the screen. It resembled distorted angry facial expressions and twisted limbs.

With a bite of his bottom lip, Jonathan typed in a prompt, ordering the entity: "Show yourself, NOW."

The screen went dark for a heartbeat, then exploded with images, a cacophony of screams, laughter, and haunting whispers as though the sounds were inside his head. An overwhelming sense of dread coursed through Jonathan's veins. *Oh fuck, what have I done?*

The faces twisted in agony as their mouths seemed to unleash silent screams. He was mesmerized by the display, even as a part of him screamed for some reason. But then, it happened.

The program shifted again, and one face emerged, clearer than the rest, its eyes piercing through the digital mess, locking onto Jonathan's eyes and drawing him in. It smiled a cruel, mocking, sinister grin.

Jonathan fell back off his chair onto the wooden floor of his living room, his heart pounding so hard and fast it felt like it was going to pop out his chest. The lights in the room flickered as an unnatural cold swept through the air; the temperature dropped as though someone had turned on the air con as Jonathan clambered back into his chair. The face vanished from the screen, but Jonathan felt it lingering, as though it was still watching him. The atmosphere changed; the shadows in his apartment seemed to stretch, creeping toward him like living entities.

He tried to close the program, wrestling his fingers from the keyboard as he panicked, but it was too late. He could feel a connection pulling him into what he had summoned. He leapt up from his desk in a panic as sweat rolled down his forehead. As he wiped the sweat away, he ran over to the computer's power source and pulled the plug.

The room stood in total darkness for a few seconds before Jonathan flicked on the lights. He walked into his small kitchen and pulled open the fridge, grabbing a bottle of water and downing it in one.

Over the following days, Jonathan's life spiraled into a living nightmare. Whispers haunted him in the silence, as he tried to ignore them. He began to see transient silhouettes in the corners of his vision, dark figures that flickered on and off like static on a broken screen. Each night, he felt a weight pressing down on him, an invisible force that made him dread the fall of darkness.

He visited his doctor the next day, who diagnosed him with stress, and that all this nonsense during the night was down to sleep paralysis. Jonathan knew this wasn't the case, but he wasn't about to tell his doctor about the deep dark web. Desperate for real answers, he returned to The Dark Abyss, scrolling through the forums for any signs of comfort or answers.

He found a handful of users who spoke of similar experiences, but their stories ended in disarray, lives consumed by the entities that they had foolishly invited into our world. It was clear to Jonathan that the line between reality and the digital realm had blurred... and he was trapped in the in-between.

One night, the scary shadows in his apartment grew louder. His heart raced as the whispers became coherent, forming words that scraped at the edges of his sanity, begging him to join them.

"Join us, Jonathan," they hissed, promising power, knowledge, everything he had ever desired. "Set us free, Jonathan." The whispers grew louder, then they began shouting, then the shouting became screams, as Jonathan held his hands to his ears. Then in a moment of sheer will, Jonathan decided he needed to confront the terror he had unleashed.

Plucking up what little courage he had left, he returned to the site of the experiment, determined to erase the connection forever. But when he logged into The Forever, the page seemed altered, more malevolent, pulsating with a life of its own. The user known as Hugh. R. Doomed was gone. The sinister, mocking face reappeared, grinning at Jonathan wider than before, eyes glinting with malice.

"You think you can stop us? We are already inside you, Jonathan. We are already a part of your world now."

Panic surged through Jonathan as he felt cold fingers wrap around his throat, squeezing the air from his lungs. Realization came crashing down over him; he was not in the presence of a dark, digital entity; he had become part of it, a vessel for its dark, sinister desires and plans.

In those final moments, as darkness engulfed him, Jonathan understood that some doors should never be opened. The dark web held horrors far beyond his understanding, things that nobody should ever see, and now, they had claimed him as their own. His screams echoed into the dark void of the in-between, unheard, as he became yet another shadow lost in the depths of The Dark Abyss, a secret, whispered legend for those brave enough to step where Jonathan once did, but no one ever did... none that we know of anyway.

THE END

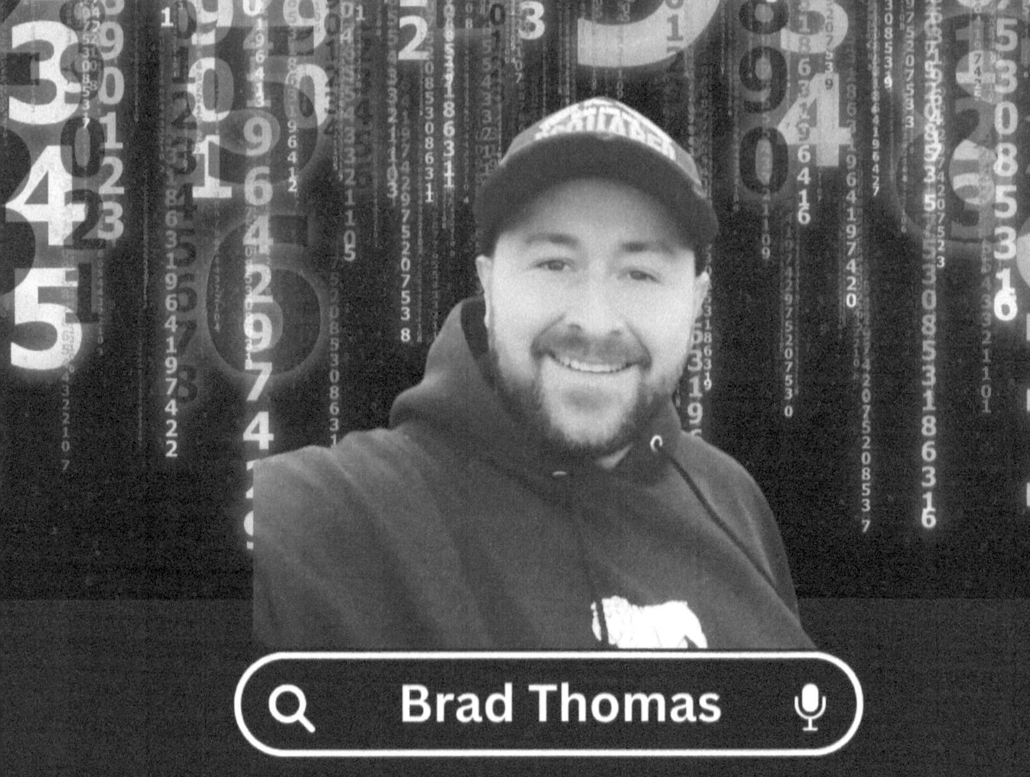

Brad Thomas is an English author of Horror, Thriller, and short stories. From a young age, all he
wanted to do was become an author. Growing up in Tipton, West Midlands, England, he never
thought it would be possible, but he never stopped chasing his dream. You can find out more about Brad's books and work on his social media.
Facebook:
https://www.facebook.com/Bradjthomaswriter
Instagram:
https://www.instagram.com/bradthomasauthor

Chapter 8
Machine

David E. Anderson

The clown got Tony first, slashing him across the throat with a meat cleaver as my friend went through the kitchen door. The flash of the blade was so fast that it took a moment for the horror to register with me.

Tony, my best friend since elementary school, spun around on staggering legs, facing the three of us, his eyes wide with disbelief. We watched with slack jaws as blood ran like a river from the gaping wound on his throat. He managed to stay on his feet, drowning in his own blood as he tried to speak.

Then his body surrendered to death, falling over sideways like a tree in a storm.

We'd been promised an exciting haunted house experience, and had been giggling when we came through the front door, not really knowing what to expect when we paid our twenty-five dollar entry fee. We were expecting a gory good time, but nothing like this.

The three of us stood frozen - Stacy, Reggie and I - as the clown stepped over his corpse. It wore a ruffled clown costume, with a plastic mask displaying a clown's face, white with a bright red nose and its unnaturally wide mouth and eyes lined with purple, and a twisted, evil grin.

Stacy and I were rooted to the spot in fear as he advanced, but Reggie broke free. He let out a raw scream and bolted for the front door. The door that had opened so easily to let us in now seemed to be welded shut. No matter how much he twisted and pulled, the door wouldn't budge.

The clown just stood there, watching us through the mask's eye holes in amusement, blood dripping from his meat cleaver.

Stacy and I finally got our shit together and turned and ran, hand in hand. Seeing Reggie struggling with the door, we went the only other way we could, up the rickety wooden steps, pulling each other along. Further into the house, yes, but what other choice did we have?

Reggie was still wrestling with the door, his sweaty hands slipping on the knob in frustration.

"Come on!" I screamed, but it was too late. The clown was swiftly approaching him, the gory cleaver raised menacingly.

Laughing, the clown drove the weapon down onto Reggie's right shoulder blade, sinking it deep with a sickening crunch. His arm dangled by a strip of flesh, swaying. Reggie's scream tore through the house.

Reggie threw a left hook into the side of the clown's face, but it didn't even seem to register, and the clown brought the blade down again, this time severing Reggie's arm entirely and sending it skidding across the blood-slicked floor.

Reggie collapsed into the fetal position, shrieking for help, but the clown merely brought the cleaver down again and again on our helpless friend.

Stacy and I didn't stop to watch the rest unfold, but bolted, our feet pounding up the stairs. My heart thundered in terror, trying to figure out how we could possibly escape.

"Caleb!" screamed Stacy. "We need to go out a window!"

The hallway stretched out before us, and I'd swear it was longer than the width of the house. Closed doors stood on either side, hiding who knows what. I didn't want to open a door and risk facing another threat. The clown was likely not the lone occupant of this house of horrors.

But we couldn't stay in the hallway. That clown could be coming upstairs at any moment.

I grabbed a random door and threw it open, and we stumbled into a child's nursery. A large wooden crib stood in the center of the room, and a rocking horse was up against a wall. The room's wallpaper was carnival-themed, with spinning wheels and colorful big tops.

I rushed to the far wall and frantically tugged at the window, but it was stuck tight. My panic was rising, and I feared meeting Reggie's fate, wasting my time trying to open something that refused to open while that damned clown closed in.

I turned away and picked up the rocking horse, hurling it at the window. The glass exploded in a shower of jagged shards, the horse falling back into the room. Finally, we had our way out.

I turned back to Stacy, and saw the clown sneaking up behind her, holding a finger to his lips as if asking me to stay quiet.

"Stacy!" I yelled, and a spear came through her stomach. The clown had traded one weapon for another. Then I realized, no, this was a different clown entirely. The mask of the first one had been lined in purple around the eyes and mouth. This one was blue. And whoever was behind the mask was heavier, with broader shoulders.

She looked at me, her eyes widening in confusion, then stared down to see the bloody tip of the spear protruding from her ruined stomach.

"Whoa," she said, her voice eerily calm, as she reached down and ran her fingers over the bloody spear tip. "This is so cool!"

"Does it hurt?" I asked. "Looks like it hurts."

She shook her head slowly, dazed. "No... Not really."

The clown yanked the spear back through her body with a sickening sound, and she collapsed to the floor and died. The clown winked at me. How it winked when it simply wore a plastic mask, I can't say. But it did. Some kind of animatronics? It was definitely the mask winking, not the eye behind it.

I scrambled through the shattered window, broken glass tearing at my skin as I squeezed through. Stacy was right; this didn't hurt at all. I could feel the glass cutting at my skin, but it was more of a tingling sensation than anything else. *How did they do this?*

I tumbled out, slamming into the ground about fifteen below, but though I could feel the impact and the air left my lungs in a rush, this didn't hurt, either.

As I got to my feet, the world spun before me. I glanced up, and saw the clown leaning out the window, its plastic grin glowing in the moonlight. It raised a hand, wiggling its fingers in a friendly wave.

I flipped him the bird, praying he wouldn't come out after me.

But he didn't need to. I heard feet crunching on the fallen leaves surrounding the house. Knowing I was done for, I turned.

Four more clowns surrounded me, all carrying various weapons - a pitchfork, a machete, a butcher's knife and a lead pipe, all wearing the same type of mask and outfit, but different colors.

I backed against the side of the house, thinking *'no fair!'* How could there be six of them? Did one recruit the others? This didn't make any sense, but I supposed it didn't have to.

Horror movies were fun, but they were bullshit.

The clowns closed in, ripping and stabbing at me. I fought back as hard as I could, but I was unarmed, just throwing ineffective punches. And before I knew it, I was dead, just like Tony, Reggie and Stacy.

A tingling sensation spread through my body, like an electric current. My eyes fluttered open and I took a deep breath, yanking off the headset which covered my eyes. My living room came into focus, my friends appearing in three boxes on my monitor, and I was in the fourth, staring forward at the camera above my computer.

That had been intense, like the most vivid dream ever. I'd played plenty of VR games in my days, but this was way beyond next level, exactly as the website had promised. Hell, this was beyond whatever was beyond the next level, and likely beyond that.

My friends had already taken off their headsets and were excitedly discussing what had happened, like we'd just gotten off a thrilling rollercoaster ride rather than watching each other be brutally murdered.

...felt so real...how did they DO that?...shit, we were in a horror movie!...

Their voices rang in my ears, but I could barely hear them. The tingling slowly faded away. I glanced down at the headset in my hands, dark and sleek, with tiny metal pins lining the inside. They were too small to puncture my skin, barely noticeable when I put it on, but when I pressed the button and the helmet tightened, I'd felt them pressing against my skin uncomfortably.

"Hey, you okay, Caleb?" Stacy's voice cut through my daze. I looked up at her smiling face on the monitor. She was Reggie's ex-girlfriend, and we were kind of dating now. Nothing serious, mostly just hanging out as friends with the occasional hookup, which I don't think Reggie knew about quite yet.

"Caleb?" asked Tony. "You there, man?"

I had to admit it had been a thrilling experience. We all dug horror movies, and getting to experience something like that was out of this world. But a lingering unease crawled up my spine.

"Yeah," I said. "It's just. This...shouldn't exist. Not yet."

Reggie laughed. "Okay, but obviously it does. And it's awesome!"

"Totally," Stacy chimed in. "I could feel that spear going right through me, and—"

"Whoa!" Reggie's eyes widened. "You got a spear through you?"

"Yeah."

"I saw it on the screen," said Tony excitedly. "It was gnarly as hell."

"I could feel it," said Stacy, "but it didn't hurt. Why didn't it hurt?"

"Because it's not supposed to," said Tony with a hint of authority. He was the one who'd found out about the website, the one who dragged us into this. "If it actually caused pain, no one would want to play the game. But everything else was real, just like they promised. I knew we couldn't get hurt, but when that clown slashed my throat... For a second, I swore something had gone wrong, that I was a goner. It was freaky."

"Yeah," agreed Reggie, his grin faltering. "I thought I was really dying there when my arm came off. I expected, like, some phantom pain at least. A psychological sting. But nope - just felt like pins and needles. Weird"

"So we going in again?" Stacy had a flicker of excitement in her eyes.

"Hell, yeah!" Reggie pumped his fist. "This trip's on me!"

Their excitement was contagious, even as I debated whether to join them. This website delivered everything it promised—a horror experience that was practically indistinguishable from reality. The only thing missing was the pain.

The headsets were three hundred dollars a pop, and each trip into the VR world was ten bucks a person, or twenty-five for a group of up to four. Each horror-themed adventure lasted up to ten minutes. Slashers, zombie apocalypse, haunted asylum, various types of monsters you could fight. Why wouldn't they give a more pleasant option for those who weren't into horror, but wanted to try out this next-level VR?

The tech was advanced—too advanced. Had it even been tested? I mean, really tested? Could something this immersive, this real, cause some kind of psychological break in people?

And the setup didn't make sense either. We'd all downloaded a small software package and the headsets just plugged into our computers' USB ports. So how the fuck was this system being powered? You'd think it would require its own console at the very least.

"You in, Caleb?" asked Stacy, starting to pull her helmet over her head.

"Yeah," I muttered, forcing a smile. "Sure."

"You don't sound so enthusiastic," said Tony, chuckling.

"This whole thing...it just doesn't add up." I tossed my helmet up and down in my hands a couple of times, trying to psych myself up for another round.

"What doesn't add up?" asked Reggie.

I knew that if I explained further, they'd accuse me of overthinking things. We'd gone in, it had been awesome, and we got out okay. What more is there to say?

"Never mind," I said. "Let's do this."

I took a deep breath, slipped the headset on, and my finger hovered over the power button that was on the USB cord.

I watched as my friends pressed their buttons, watched the LED panels on the front light up, watched the helmet tighten almost as if molding to their scalps.

I couldn't do it. Something was wrong. I took my helmet off. "Hey, guys?"

No response. They were already gone, deep in the other world. I don't even know what kind of horror experience they'd gone into. Tony was primary in our group, so he set the destination.

Either way, they were beyond being able to hear me.

I doubted this website, and what they're doing, was legal. Tony had found out about it in some online horror movie group, and said that the website didn't do any kind of promotion, but just survived on word of mouth. Given the insane level of tech involved, this should already be the next big thing, so why hadn't I heard about it? Were they even profiting off their tech? Why was it just a thinly-kept secret?

I sat there, staring at the screen where my friends appeared in neat little boxes, unmoving. Basically in hibernation. I assumed I could still join them on this adventure. We got through the first one okay. But since everything about this filled me with dread, I didn't want to keep doing it. I'd have to figure out a way to get them to stop somehow, before... I don't know. Something was going to happen, eventually. I could feel it.

Minutes passed, and I kept expecting one of them to wake up. In our first adventure, Tony's death happened pretty quick. We were maybe three minutes into the game when his throat was slit by that wicked clown. But now five minutes had ticked by, per the timer on the screen, and they were all still asleep. Still locked in the game.

Hold on, Tony said that he'd been watching on the screen when Stacy got impaled. So shouldn't I be able to see their adventure on my screen? Or was I only allowed to view the events after I left the scenario?

I kept waiting for someone to wake up. Six minutes passed. Seven.

"Goddamnit, wake up," I muttered, and I could hear the panic in my voice. "Someone wake up!"

According to the website, the games were designed to last under ten minutes. But that didn't guarantee they would end that quickly, I guess. A particularly good player might survive longer.

But we were all newbies, inexperienced.

Someone should have died by now.

Ten minutes passed. When it got to eleven, my pulse was racing. I knew talking to them was pointless. They couldn't hear me, not unless I fired up my helmet and went inside. But maybe somebody on the website was listening in. Monitoring the game. Maybe they could help me get them out.

I grabbed my headset and turned it on, leaving it on the desk in front of me.

"Is anyone there?" I asked. "My friends have been in the game too long. Can't you end it? I'm getting worried."

A voice came through my speaker. It was calm, emotionless. "Put the headset on, Caleb."

I briefly wondered how he knew my name, but figured Tony had given it when he signed us up.

"Ummm, no. Something's gone wrong. Just stop the game. They've been in for almost twelve minutes. Games aren't supposed to go that long."

"Caleb?" the voice asked.

"Yes?"

"I need you to listen very carefully to what I'm about to say."

"Yeah, yeah. I'm listening."

"Put your headset on, or I kill one of your friends."

"Don't you get it? I *want* you to kill them. Get 'em out of..." Then it hit me. "Wait, what are you talking about? Kill them...how?"

"Would you like a demonstration? Pick one."

My blood ran cold. "No... Why would you do that? We're paying customers!"

"Either put the helmet on...or choose who dies."

I looked around the room, not sure for what. Answers, maybe. "I'm calling 911!" I said in a threatening tone.

"You do that, and they all die," the voice responded smoothly. "Put the helmet on, Caleb. Right now."

Stacy lived just down the street from me, about a block away. I could run to her house, unplug her computer. Get her out.

And I had no doubt they'd respond by killing Tony and Reggie.

"You're bluffing," I said, trying to sound more confident that I felt. "No way does your system have enough power to kill someone over the internet."

"I'm getting bored, Caleb, and I don't like being bored. Pick one. Pick who I use to demonstrate what we're capable of. If I'm bluffing, you have nothing to worry about, right? So go ahead and pick one. Go ahead and call my bluff."

My mouth went dry. He left me no choice. I either had to enter the game, or pick one and hope he truly was bluffing. So I made my choice.

"Alright, asshole. Kill Reggie. Show me."

I really didn't believe they could do it. But just in case, I picked the one I knew the least. He was more Tony's friend than mine. I'd only hung out with him a few times. Seemed nice, but he was one of those guys who only did something for you if he wanted something in return. And, frankly, I suspected Stacy still pined for him a bit. Not that I wanted him dead, but he just seemed like the choice where I'd lose the least.

Reggie started jerking violently, as if being riddled with bullets, or maybe electrocuted. His head started snapping back as if struck by invisible blows. His mouth opened in a silent scream, and I could see smoke curling upward his headset. Made me think of someone in an electric chair.

"Stop! Stop!" I shouted, my voice cracking, but got no answer. The convulsions went on and on for what felt like minutes, until Reggie's body finally stopped and slumped sideways out of his chair, out of the view of the camera. His helmet had gone dark, but was still strapped to his head.

"Put your headset on, Caleb," said the voice. "Don't make me ask again."

My hands shook as I lifted the headset and slipped it on. I wished to God we'd never heard of this website. I pressed the power button on the cord and felt the helmet tightening.

I found myself standing on the edge of a murky moat, staring through the rain at a castle on the other side. Dark clouds churned overhead, spitting flashes of lightning. Loud thunder boomed from the heavens.

The castle was massive, its blackened stone walls stretching upward, with towers rising above like jagged teeth.

A wooden drawbridge led across the moat towards a pair of enormous doors that stood ajar, waiting for me.

I tried to steady my breathing. This was something out of an old monster movie. Frankenstein? Dracula? As much as I didn't want to face whatever lay inside the depths of that wicked castle, I had no doubt the others had gone inside.

They would have crossed that bridge without a second thought. Why wouldn't they? That was the adventure, right? They had no reason to see the castle as any more dangerous than that house of psychotic clowns.

But I knew better now. The real monsters weren't lurking inside that castle—they were the ones controlling them.

My instincts said to turn and run. Abandon them while I still had the chance. But if I turned and fled, where would I go? How could I escape from this game, except by dying in it?

Death was, ironically, the only way to survive.

So I headed across the drawbridge towards that old castle, getting more and more terrified with each step, expecting Frankenstein to appear and start shuffling towards me, arms outstretched, or Dracula gliding through the night, his fangs bared.

But I arrived inside the castle undisturbed. The doors didn't slam shut behind me, and no creatures of the night popped out of the shadows.

I found myself in a vast stone hall, the walls adorned with lit torches, held on by metal brackets.

Several stone archways led off in various directions, making me think of huge mouths waiting to swallow me whole

"Come on," I muttered under my breath. "Do something." I'm not sure if I was talking to myself, or the game.

A scream pierced the air, a gut-wrenching cry that made me almost jump out of my skin. A male voice, seeming to come from an open doorway to my right, which led to a spiraling stone staircase, heading down.

I headed over to that staircase. Because of the curve, I couldn't see all the way to the bottom. I glanced back to make sure Dracula wasn't sneaking up on me, then called down. I could hear moans from below, people in terrible pain. "Hello?"

"Who's there?" called a voice, male. Familiar. Wait, was that...?

"Reggie?" I asked, my heart hammering as I started down the stone steps.

"Caleb! Jesus, man! Don't come down here!"

"Caleb?" asked another voice. Stacy. "Go back!"

"How are you alive, Reggie?" I yelled in confusion.

"What do you mean?" he asked.

"I saw you die!"

"What are you talking about?" Reggie's voice wavered in confusion.

I stopped walking, my mind reeling. I saw the convulsions, the blood, the smoking headset. He couldn't have survived all of that. Perhaps it was some kind of CGI trick - realistic illusions were obviously not beyond their capabilities - but I didn't think so.

Reggie was dead.

So how...

Then it hit me.

He was dead, all right. But only in the real world. This place, this digital nightmare, played by different rules. Here, life and death had other meanings.

I finally reached the bottom of the stairs and came out into a dungeon, my breath catching in my throat at the sight before me.

My friends stood upright, their bodies stiff, suspended by a strange concoction of green metal spheres, pipes and wires. I struggled to make sense of what I saw.

The spheres made a chugging sound, and I realized they were engines of some kind. Doing what, though, I couldn't say. Wisps of steam rose from them, and I thought I could hear something traveling from the engines through the pipes, which disappeared into the floor and walls.

Tony, Stacy and Reggie—each one was crying and quivering, their faces twisted in pain. They were connected to those spherical engines through wires about as thick as yarn. The wires were green, like the spheres, but when they came close to my friends' bodies, they became flesh-colored. No, not flesh-colored, but actual flesh. The flesh from their arms, chests and bodies had merged with the wires, becoming one.

I walked toward Stacy, trying to figure out a way to free her. How could I separate her from the wires, if she was part of the wires?

"Caleb, stop," Stacy whimpered, her voice ragged. "Don't come closer. It'll get you, too!"

I ignored her and rushed to her side, grabbing at one of the wires and trying to yank it from her. As soon as I did, she let out a terrible scream of agony. "Stop! That hurts!"

"What do I do?" I shouted, my voice trembling in panic. Every instinct said to get the hell out of here, but I couldn't leave them like this.

"Just leave," she begged. "Please, Caleb, just go!"

"Not without you," I promised, though I knew I had no idea of how to free her from this strange captivity.

She looked past me with fear rising in her eyes. "Caleb!"

I spun around just in time to see one of those green engines rising from the floor about a foot away from me, pushed up by a pipe like a periscope rising from the water.

The engine whirred and sputtered, then a green wire shot out with a snapping sound, embedding itself into my right arm.

Pain flared as I tried to yank it free, but I felt my muscles growing weak, like energy was being drained through the wire. The flesh of my arm stretched along the length of the cord, towards the machine.

A second engine rose, and another wire embedded itself into my chest. The process repeated, the skin pulled taut, merging with the wire until it became one thing.

I gasped, remembering how there was no pain in the first game, and wondering why it wasn't so now.

A third engine rose on a pipe, and this time the cord went into my forehead. I felt an electric jolt, then could feel something vital being sucked out. Not blood, no. Something much deeper than that.

Energy? Fear?

All I knew was that my body was being devoured.

And let me tell you, it hurt like fucking hell.

David E. Anderson grew up in the '70s, loving Godzilla movies and the "Night Stalker" series, developing a love for horror early on. As a teenager, he immersed himself in the books by the likes of Stephen King, F. Paul Wilson and Dean Koontz, and wanted to try his hand at what they do so well. He wrote his first novel, "The Void," in his mid-teens, followed by six more—three of which he's self-published. Watch for news about his debut novel, SWEET DREAMS, coming spring 2025!

Chapter 9
Through the Screen Darkly
Bert Lestrange

"Who controls the past, controls the future. Who controls the present controls the past." - George Orwell

"Those who would give up essential Liberty, to purchase a little temporary Safety, deserve neither Liberty nor Safety." -Benjamin Franklinstein

"Don't believe everything you read on the internet just because there's a picture with a quote beside it. Blaze 'em if you got 'em boys. We 'bout to fuck this Bitches all kinda up." -Abraham Lincoln, probably

The harsh computer screen's glow added the shadow of years to his steadily creasing brow. At 31, David shouldn't look or feel this old. But the endless barrage of emails, notifications, and deadlines infected every moment of his life; draining all joy until only the rancorous husk of purpose remained. The monotony of the new "middle class" was a slow and marching death; each passing day another nail in the coffin housing his soul.

Rubbing his strained eyes and considering his fraying sanity, David glanced at the clock. 7:42 pm. Another late night, well beyond his government mandated 50-hour work week and yet another float in the parade of broken promises to himself. Hadn't that been his New Year's Resolution? It hadn't lasted through the first week in January. He wasn't appreciated by his company. Hell, he wasn't even a priority to himself.

"Screw it." David sighed, saving his work before shutting down the laptop.

Snatching up his coat, he grumbled his way through the forest of cubicles, down the elevator, and trudged into the night. A bitter gust of frigid air slapped him awake, stealing his breath. But it was good. Just being outside, even if "outside" was a grey, metropolitan wasteland, entirely devoid of the verdant green of the real world.

His governmentally mandated electric car was in a garage half a mile away. Private parking within the city was just one "benefit" the company offered along with bulk coffee at only $1 a cup.

His fingers were numb on the wheel and he spent a few minutes warming them at the vents before joining an endless sea of blaring horns, squealing brakes, and shouting drivers. Generally, rush hour traffic was long gone, but the radio offered the explanation of a nasty wreck at a well-known bottleneck. Two-hour delay expected, stay tuned! More to come from WBBL.

His stomach rumbled.

Frustration flared and he decided to treat himself for a change. This, he promised himself, would be the beginning of a new chapter. For real this time.

Pulling up the search engine on his phone, he found a nearby BYOB pizza joint that was open until ten. The name was oddly nostalgic of too many nights with too many drinks, of making good memories with people he'd never remember. Had that really been more than half a decade ago? When was the last time he'd spent time with anyone other than coworkers?

"Da Vinci's Pizzeria, what can we put on your edible art?" David could hear the pale, pimpled face in the worker's cracking voice.

"I'll take the meat pizza. Large. A dozen wings with Cajun dust. Ah, hell, why not toss in a cinnamon sticks as well. Extra icing. Uh… I think that's it."

David's mouth watered at the thought of each greasy, cheesy, decadent bite. He should have done this months ago. Maybe once a month he'd treat himself. Once a paycheck, even.

Buttons clicked on the line's other end. "Ok, I got it all put in. Is the address on file still good for billing?"

"Yep. And I'd like it delivered. I'll pay whatever, but I'm stuck in traffic. Could it be scheduled for… like… an hour from now?" He asked.

There was a short pause. "Sir, we don't really schedule drivers. You could call back later if you'd like, but we stop taking delivery requests at 8:30."

David eyed the clock on his dash which read 8:26 pm.

"Nah, bud. Just get it there and I'll nuke it if needed."

There was a long sigh of annoyance from the teen. "Cool. that's $76.51."

David swore.

"You gotta be shitting me. Are you kidding?"

Now he heard the kid's smirk, braces and all. "No sir. The Heart Stopper Meat Locker is $32 for a large, Da Vinci's hand-crafted wings are $20 a dozen, premium Cajun dust is $3.50, the Munchy Cinnabox is $15. Icing is two bucks a cup. Oh dang, I forgot the delivery fee. So, add a flat $15 to that. Plus tip."

"You charge for wing seasoning? If I'm paying $15 for a delivery, why am I also expected to tip? What the Hell is 'hand crafted' about your wings?" He was getting hangry and realized it a sentence too late.

There was a degree of self-righteous condescension in his canned response that only pissy teenagers are capable of. "Sir, if you can't afford it, you could trim the order. In these modern times, the price of goods is steadily rising. We here at Da Vinci's hold our ingredients and ourselves to the highest standards. While it may cost a little more, we think-"

"Sure, whatever. Yeah. Send them to the house and I'll send $100. They can keep the rest." I was exasperated and my stomach felt like it was eating itself.

There was another long pause. "Sir, $9 is hardly an appropriate tip on a $91 order. And technically we're after delivery order acceptance hours, so."

His clock read 8:30 pm.

"Fuck it. I'll send $120, just put the goddamn pizza on my door step, ok?"

"Yes Sir. I'll send the invoice to this number. We'll be on our way soon! Thanks for ca-"

David ended the call, fuming, and punched the steering wheel.

His phone buzzed and he approved the charge. Traffic had finally started picking up and he almost felt bad about his outburst. Almost.

His phone buzzed again. Then three more times. The road again ground to a halt as another ambulance shrieked past.

Sighing, David checked his messages and found the following:

"Health Insurance Alert: Premium increased to protect your health. Reason noted: High-Risk Food choice including: Pizza, Greasy. Dessert, Baked. Misc High Fat/sodium Option. Choose healthier options to reduce our costs and yours!"

His stomach sank. Oh shit.

He'd forgotten about the wildly unpopular legislation implemented about a year before. After purchasing unlimited rights to Ancestry.com, 23&Me, and 27 other global genetic databases, the United States Government quickly pushed through a single payer health-care system. In this way, they could use genetic disposition and propensity to charge each customer based on individual genetic propensity rather than blanket pricing. It was supposedly intended to decrease average costs, but even as a mostly healthy person, David's premium had doubled. It took no time to absorb all domestic phone companies, energy producers, grocery stores, and fast-food chains into a collectively oppressive conglomerate. In just under two years, the government had slithered its tendrils into every aspect of American life.

"Auto Insurance Alert: Premium increased to protect other drivers. Reason noted: Phone activity while driving. Arrive alive, don't text and drive!"

"Health Insurance Alert: Premium increased to protect your health. Reason noted: Inappropriate Anger Response anonymously reported (Phone Call). A visit with a mental health practitioner in your area has been made for April 6 @ 8:15 am. Costs will be automatically withdrawn from your account. It's ok to not be ok. We're here to help!"

"Notification of order override. (3) items substituted: (1) The Heart Stopper Meat Locker (large): Organic Vegetarian toppings with high fiber crust (medium), (2) Da Vinci's Wings: Removed/No Substitute, (3) Munchy Cinnabox: Removed/No Substitute. Your health is our business!"

Son of a bitch... They hadn't even asked... They just changed it... He wondered if they'd "automatically" reduced his costs. Not likely.

By the time David pulled into his driveway, his anger had turned into a deep, leaden despair. He stumbled to his front door, footsteps echoing through the empty night. The pizza was waiting for him at the doorstep, its warmth, like his enthusiasm for it, long gone, replaced by the cold hatred of what his life had become.

He carried the single box inside, movements mechanical and robotic. The house was dark, silent, otherwise devoid of life. He didn't bother turning on the lights. What was the point? It was just him and the cold, tasteless pizza, a bitter reminder of everything wrong in this world.

David sank into the couch, the pizza box resting on his lap. He opened it and stared at the sad, wilted vegetables, mostly cauliflower, spinach, and carrots, scattered over what appeared to be a thin, wicker basket crust. It mocked him like a cruel joke from a dark, faceless god. He couldn't bring himself to eat it.

It wasn't just him. The whole country had fallen for the rouse. A two-party system controlled by the same key players, intent on total control of the population. He was nothing more than a cog in the machine; reduced to a series of algorithms and data points. It was so obvious now.

David opened his eyes and stared at the dark ceiling, manifesting swirling nightmares from the shadows above. The silence was suffocating, pressing down on him like a physical weight. He felt trapped, not just in his house, but in his life. The walls were closing in, and he was powerless to stop it.

Weeks passed, possibly months. It was hard to tell from his cubicle as each day was a mirror of the previous. With his increased costs, the long hours became necessarily longer. It came to pass he spent more time at work than at home. That didn't really matter. He had no partner, no kids, no friends. Not even an asshole cat to piss on his pillow while he was out. He was all alone.

Drowning in his own misery, he didn't notice the figure wearing a wooden sign covered with anti-government propaganda. The woman snatched his coat pocket and pulled him back.

"Freedom is so close, my friend. Look and see. Look and see!" The woman whirled, releasing colorful pamphlets as she spun.

Dozens fell to the ground as she laughed and called to the crowd one at a time before quickly switching targets.

"Has your insurance gotten cheaper? Are you healthier? Do you remember optional 40-hour work weeks?"

Then, she spun back to him, meeting his eyes. He couldn't look away from her madness.

"When was the last time you had a goddamn pepperoni pizza without paying out the ass for it?"

He held her gaze and felt the spark of a connection. She reached out her hand, flyer between index and forefinger. David reached out trembling fingers to grab it.

But his hand went white-hot with a flare of pain, then instantly numb.

Looking up, David had just enough time to see the first of eight officers rugby tackle the woman, signs and all, to the ground. Her head sounded like a melon as it bounced on the asphalt, but that didn't stop the others from taking their own cheap shots. Two of them kept passersby at bay while two more picked up her pamphlets. One older gentleman took a tazer to the ribs when he initially refused to give up a green one he'd collected. "Stop resisting!" one shouted before discharging a second tazer against his neck. He was promptly cuffed and manhandled into the same police car as the unconscious dissenter. She was bleeding from one ear.

The crowed muttered among themselves as the officers drove off without even a single word. All of them seemed to be having difficulty understanding the blitzkrieg "justice" they'd just witnessed. David's hand was already bruising before he realized one of the cops must have struck him with a baton.

By the time he arrived at work, two things were self-evident: there was no way he'd be able to modify data points with any reasonable speed and his hand was probably broken.

After a short discussion with his boss, he was sent home with instructions not to return until he'd been properly evaluated. But before he even left the building, his phone buzzed.

"Health Insurance Alert: Employer reported injury (non-work related). An appointment has been made for you with a local physician on June 29 @ 5:00 pm. Premium increased to protect your health. Your health is our business!"

June 29? That was nearly a month away. What was he supposed to do until then? David had been living paycheck to paycheck as it was, using a credit card to bridge the two, and still just barely getting by. This would financially cripple him.

Taking a deep breath, he opened his car door and just sat there. What the Hell was he going to do? He sat there, too stunned to think. After ten minutes, he turned the key and immediately his phone buzzed twice.

"Health Insurance Alert: Premium increased to protect your health. Reason noted: Operating heavy machinery with a major injury."

"Auto Insurance Alert: Premium increased to protect other drivers. Reason noted: Operating a vehicle with a major injury."

He howled. "That's not fucking fair! You can't double dip! You wet totalitarian abortion. Fuck you!"

David threw the phone against his windshield, cracking both in the process.

He patted his pockets with his good hand. It was a long-forgotten habit from his college days, back before cigarettes were banned. He hadn't smoked in five years.

A teal pamphlet crumpled against his fingers. Slowly revealing it, David remembered the curious woman who must have stuffed it in before being brutalized. He hadn't even realized what she'd done and wondered if she was ok. The folded paper was just bold, black text on the front. The message was surprisingly simple.

STOP THE CORRUPTION!

Tired of dictatorial oppression?

Do you miss eating the food, driving the cars, and working the hours that you want?

Don't you remember when things were affordable?

BUT THERE IS HOPE!

The DARK WEB is the answer you seek. The Dark Web is your digital savior!

As he flipped the flier over and found a mini-SD card taped in place that read "Insert Before Powering On" in tiny letters.

Any other day, he'd have assumed it was a virus, but David had seen what the woman went through to deliver her message. His bank account was probably in the negative, his sanity was paper thin, and his life was about to be in shambles. He decided to give it a shot. After all, what could they possibly steal?

Back at home, he followed the instructions. Powering off his government approved home laptop and ignoring his government issued phone, he plugged in the contraband SD card and rebooted.

The machine's fans whirred, struggling for about thirty seconds before the screen lit up. Notably, the little orange camera light, which was always on, remained dark. Rather than its usual logo and loading screen, a yellow smiling emoji face with X's for eyes grinned back at him along with words beneath.

Are you alone? Yes/No

David clicked "Yes".

Are you in a safe place? Yes/No

"Yes"

Are you ready to take back your life? Yes/No

"Abso-fucking-lutely." He whispered before clicking "Yes".

Welcome to the Dark Web Revolution, friend.

Instead of his personalized background, his laptop showed a bookshelf. Each volume had a clickable name.

Gray's Anatomy: Healthcare

Cobra Handbook: Wealthcare

Utopia: Selfcare

Jurassic Park: Genetic Record Modulation

The Republic: Unmonitored Discussion Boards

It seemed too good to be true, but David was too fascinated and beaten down to look away. Clicking on "Utopia", he fell headfirst down the first of many rabbit holes.

David didn't honestly believe it until the pizza arrived. He found "Freedom of Food" under the Utopia header and ignored the rest temporarily. No mention of brand or payment, he simply clicked options from a list and the hot, greasy meat-covered goodness arrived within half an hour. The driver knocked and by the time he could answer the door, the black muscle car was already driving away.

It was the best thing he'd ever eaten.

His phone remained mute on the subject.

That emboldened him, scheduling a visit later that day with a mobile physician for his hand. Shortly after lunch, a doctor, or at least a reasonable facsimile, arrived with a mobile x-ray unit.

David asked a lot of questions, but the pretty doctor just smiled and avoided everything except medical matters. She didn't acknowledge any question even vaguely regarding the Dark Web Resistance.

The were fractures in several of the small carpal bones in mid-hand area, but nothing critical. They would heal in 3-4 weeks, but needed to be immobilized for best results. She didn't offer her name or wear a nametag, but the doctor used a sort of soaking plaster to set it before leaving.

"How do I pay you?" David asked as she picked up the last of her supplies and moved toward the door.

She paused, back stiffening momentarily, but didn't look back. "Sir, the freedom of healthcare is its own reward."

Later, while browsing, he found the alcohol section. Brands which had been banned for more than a year were readily available, including Jack Daniel's, Svedka, and Jose Cuervo. He kept waiting for the rug to be jerked from beneath him, but there was no prompt to input credit card information and no prices listed anywhere. The order was limited to one bottle, but he opted for a classic: Buffalo Trace Straight Bourbon. There was an option to add cigarettes or marijuana by the single, pack, or carton. He'd never been a pot smoker, but accepted anyway. It couldn't hurt to try a little weed, right?

Just as with the pizza, it arrived at his doorstep in just under an hour, but this time he never saw the driver or car.

He poured the medium amber liquid over a couple of ice cubes in wonder. Savoring the smell (caramel, butterscotch, and something like pumpkin spice) he took a small sip. The taste was reminiscent of toffee and candied fruit, but not too sweet. In short, it was divine. Hiding the bottle behind his refrigerator, he returned to the computer. His hand throbbed a little less.

Browsing the comically named Jurassic Park header, he was shocked to find a free service which claimed to modify your governmental genetic profile within their database. Doing so, should reduce his healthcare premiums and car insurance costs while opening new avenues for food services. AI monitored the information, it explained, and the changes wouldn't be noticed outside of a massive audit.

After his previous successes, he boldly added his name, social security number, and genetic identification number. The response seemed positive, though it would be a gradual change to reduce the inherent risks of such manipulation, which was a major felony (Defrauding a Governmental Agency).

Chuckling, he delved deeper into Utopia.

This proved his first off-putting experience. Pornography had been banned and sites offering it subsequently removed from all available search engines. Here, he found everything he could imagine and then some. But among the categories were "very young", "snuff", and "mutilation". Just reading the terms made him physically ill.

He finished the bourbon and backed out to the main menu before retrieving his bottle and pouring another to settle his stomach and decided to try his smokes. Thankfully, his little farmhouse still had half an acre of forest behind it. The neighbors were out of sight and out of mind. Not that anyone went outside much these days, but it was still a comfort.

When he'd purchased the home, it had come with twelve acres of unrestricted, untouched forest. But after the Nature Preservation Act, no single household was allowed to hold more than half an acre at a time. The government "generously" purchased his "excess property" at just under a thousand dollars per acre. He took the offer because the overtly mentioned alternative was losing it without recompense to Advanced Eminent Domain.

Climate change was certainly real, science had proved it a thousand times over, but the abusive practices in its name were suffocating. He remained one of the few allowed to keep a car because the nearest public transportation routes were a prohibitive distance away. He missed his truck, but the barebones electric model wasn't so bad. At least he didn't have to buy gas anymore. Some of his colleagues walked two miles to the nearest stop each day.

The joints came in a package reminiscent of cigarettes with a pouch on the side dedicated to an included lighter. It was an old school Bic model with a thumb operated sparker. It took a few tries before his fingers remembered how to ignite it.

The first small drag was bitter and earthy, not entirely unpleasant. But the second, braver pull sent him into a coughing fit. He took his time with it, savoring the banned substance, somehow better because of its illicit nature. For lack of a better word, David felt slightly turned on by the mischief of it. And, for the first time in years, he regretted living alone.

His last relationship was a quick, spicy fling with a handsome older man who was far more worldly than himself. It ended when the gentleman's wife found their text conversations. Six months later, homosexuality was criminalized under the "American Family Preservation Initiative".

David sighed contentedly, feeling the effects kick in. His brain felt a little fuzzy and warm, like it was wearing a cozy sweater. His forehead felt "tall", like it should be somewhere around the roofline. That seemed hilarious and he doubled over with laughter.

Now his whole body had that "cozy sweater" sensation and his arms were suddenly quite heavy. He practically danced back to his computer. The odd, unfamiliar feeling was exhilarating and he realized all at once that he was happy. His cheeks ached from grinning. The muscles weren't used to it.

David clicked on The Republic, finding message boards and forums dedicated to everything from how to grow your own food (a major misdemeanor) to fiery rants about the "United States of Authoritarianism".

Even in the haze of euphoria, the unsettling concerns remained regarding what he'd seen. "Very young". How was it possible for something as wonderful and benevolent as this could offer such evil with only a click? The duality of man is truly a horrific thing.

Later, he'd find listings for hard drugs: Heroin, Cocaine, and something called "Snarfle" which promised an existential awakening somewhere between DMT and Mescaline. David would stumble upon disturbing delivery services for exotic pets, human slaves, assisted suicide, and live stream torture/sex chambers.

But at the moment, he was content to drink bourbon, smoke grass, and watch consenting adults fuck each other.

Curious, and emboldened by strong drink after months of sobriety, he clicked on the "Red Room" link. It sent him to a portal with several live feed links. One showed a beautiful young woman in the thumbnail, big beautiful blue eyes, skin like pale honey. Great figure, curves in all the right places with a waist that would make Barbie jealous. She was exactly the kind of girl he'd dreamed of before his experimentation with men. His hand was on his cock and stroking before he even opened the stream.

There were dozens of people in chat, some offering outrageous sums of money for... something. A live bidding war was in full force, but what was up for grabs wasn't obvious.

On the screen, a yellow light dangled above a concrete floor with a drain in the center. The gorgeous woman had been mutilated beyond recognition. One of her eyes had been removed and a gaping, bloody socket was all that remained. As he watched, unable to turn away, someone wearing a gas mask used vice grips to crush her left nipple and pull it taught. She screamed and begged, but he simply slipped a rusty hand-saw from his belt and sliced away at her breast in a jagged, ripping fashion. Blood spurted and David nearly vomited.

The auction ended, the high bidder had offered $220,500. Chat locked down the moment it closed except for his text.

Use the vicegrips on her clit, rip it out from the root. When she stops screaming, use a blowtorch. Start with her toes, crisp the skin black and keep going until her hair burns away. Take your time.

What the fuck? WHAT THE FUCKING FUCK?!

David slammed closed the laptop just as the man with the vice grips went to one knee and unplugged the SD card and flung it across the room. His stomach failed to hold back the puke that gushed from his lips.

Surely that couldn't be real. What kind of fucked up pervert could do something to another human being? This wasn't porn, it was torture.

He needed a cold shower and another shot of whiskey.

David's hand shook as he powered on the laptop, watching it flicker to life. This time without the SD card, had to appear normal from time to time. Everyone on the forums said so; it's how they catch you. Being lazy with the card, changing your routine. The eerie glow illuminated his dark bedroom, casting sinister shadows along the walls. His heart pounded with ever growing paranoia, guilt, and the disconcerting prickle on the nape of his neck that told him that he was being watched. It followed him everywhere. Like eyes crawling over his shoulder.

The orange camera light was a constant reminder.

His heart hammered his ribs, each thud a deafening reminder of the fear which had taken root within it. Could they pull his recent exploration?

It had been three weeks since he took the plunge into the murky waters of the unrestricted internet. Moral ambiguity and cheap thrills no longer seemed worth it, even if it meant freedom. Everything had changed so quickly, spiraling beyond his control. Exhilaration soon transformed to dread.

Before, his life had been stressful and draining, but now it was a waking nightmare. If he'd only been smarter with it; limited his misconduct to only a few instances here and there. But as Icarus, he'd flown too close to the Sun. Now he was forced to watch help-lessly as the world screamed toward him.

The changes came on subtly at first.

His internet speed would slow shortly after start-up, but only when he used the card. His phone battery drained twice as quickly as before and his calls had a weird clicky static in the background. His own voice seemed to echo. No matter where he went, black, unmarked cars with tinted windows seemed to be just ahead or behind.

David might have shrugged all this off as circumstantial evidence, paranoia, or a guilty conscience, but when the little camera light on his computer flickered back on, he knew he was cooked. It was in the middle of a browsing session in which he bounced between a general government hate forum and an LGBTQ+ dating thread.

The camera popped on while he'd been using the card and he froze. He tried to close the browsers, but the screen seemed frozen for perhaps ten seconds. Immediately after, the light went out and control was returned to him. He tried to convince himself that he'd imagined it, but the intense terror stuck with him even several weeks later. Since then, he'd avoided the card.

A week after joining the "Resistance", he started receiving strange messages regarding his health insurance premiums. They were decreases, but the lettering was off, sometimes jumbled or misspelled. Other times there were glitched symbols that were entirely unintelligible. It was unsettling.

After 2 weeks, he received an email with no sender, no subject, and no body, however, it had an attachment. David would eat his own car before opening that. That day was the first he'd noticed the strange cars following him. He thought it was curious at first and decided to test it. After making 4 consecutive right turns, it was still a lazy block behind.

When that one kept didn't follow as he boarded the interstate onramp, he breathed a sigh of relief. But less than a mile up the road, another nearly identical car fell in behind him and continued all the way to his house. It slowed as he pulled into the driveway, but continued on after he pulled in.

Fear gnawed at his fraying sanity like long-toothed rats. His nerves were shot. Anxiety quickly morphed into full blown panic.

Tonight, though, the black car parked at the end of his driveway and was soon met by its twin. The next time he checked, a herd of them had gathered.

David moved as quickly as he could. He snatched up the half-empty bottle of bourbon, the last two joints, half a dozen remote controlled sex toys, and even the fast-food wrappers. After shoving it all into a black trash bag, he ejected the SD card, considered it for a moment, then added the whole laptop to the mess. In the back yard leered a stone circle which was intended to be a place of marshmallow roasting and storytelling (before open flames became illegal). But now it would be a place of destruction. He tossed the bag on top of the brush and heaped what dry wood remained on top. After squirting an entire container of lighter fluid over the top, he used the Bic to set it all ablaze.

He shielded his face as the fireball bloomed to life, rising fifteen feet in the air before returning to head height. Then, he tossed the lighter in as well. It burst with an anticlimactic whistle.

David watched it blaze for what seemed like an eternity. In reality, it took under five minutes for the majority of the destruction to take hold.

Nerves had him twitching as he stumbled back into his home. If he'd thought ahead, he'd have taken a swig of the bourbon before incinerating it.

Instead, he opted for ice water and went to the window desperately hoping the cars had simply left. Just as he touched the blinds, a sharp rap-rap-rap came at the door. It startled him, sending his glass flying to shatter against the wall.

What would he do now? Fuck!

"Mr. David Toneberry, we're from the Federal Compliance Agency. We have a few questions." He didn't ask if he could come in before he and his three colleagues pressed past David.

David, a little annoyed even considering his palpating heart, frowned. "I didn't catch your name."

"I didn't give it. It's unnecessary and this investigation will be brief and efficient. We need to see your laptop. There seems to be an anomaly warranting evaluation. If you have a virus, we can eliminate it. We're here to help."

He shrugged, hands tremulous with fear and anxiety. "I... uh... trashed it a few days ago. Damn thing broke. Probably the virus, right?" He chuckled nervously and wanted to puke.

Glad for the easy explanation, David let out a sigh of relief.

"And you haven't placed an order for a new one? No consideration of turning it in for replacement or repair? That seems suspicious, David. Especially since you were using it at this location earlier today. Thats strike two, Mr. Toneberry. You understand intentionally lying to a federal agent regarding an active investigation is a felony? You're facing jail time, twenty years minimum. I'll give you one last chance to comply. Where is the laptop?"

Defeated, all hope lost, David led them to the back yard and pointed at the bonfire ring. One of the others brought his kitchen fire extinguisher and nearly emptied it on the blaze before extracting the charred remains of the computer with heat resistant gloves. If they'd planned that far ahead, they already knew exactly what they were walking into.

"And the micro-SD?" The agent asked.

He sighed. "I tossed it in too."

While the second agent bagged the laptop and returned to their cars, a third poked through the embers with a stick. "Contraband over here. Looks like a whiskey bottle and... something else?"

The lead agent stared at David, raising his eyebrows over his mirrored glasses in a question that didn't need to be voiced.

He was embarrassed to answer, but decided the truth was his best hope at minimizing the punishment that would obviously follow. Suddenly, he was reminded of the sound that pamphlet woman's head made bouncing against the sidewalk.

"Sex toys. Masturbation aids. Virtually controlled genital massagers. Lifelike anatomical replicas and a vibrating butt plug. How much trouble am I in?"

The agent shrugged. "I'm no judge, but your compliance will be taken into account. I have to ask, are you a homosexual, Mr. Toneberry?"

"I... don't really know. Before the legal change, I did have a male partner, but I haven't physically been with anyone in years. I'm trying to reform. I've taken the sensitivity training and reeducation classes." He nodded, dropping his head as though ashamed. "I like both, I guess, but I'm trying to change."

The agent eyed him through those glasses. "With a vibrating butt plug? Still, it's admirable to recognize your incorrect choice of homosexuality. Your honesty is appreciated, and I'll include it in my report. Based on what we've found, I'll need to bring you in for further questioning. You aren't being cited for anything at the moment and coming with us is not an admission of guilt. If you refuse, however, it will be interfering with an ongoing investigation. We'll be required to use force. Think clearly before responding: Will you come quietly and make this easy on all of us?"

The fourth agent, whose shoulders began roughly where David's head ended, cracked his knuckles, then his neck, before whipping out an extendable baton. In his meaty hands, it looked capable of shattering bone.

He gulped.

"No need for all that. I can follow orders. Just tell me what to do."

The brute looked disappointed.

David woke with his whole body throbbing. His hair was crusted to the sterile concrete floor with his own blood, snot, and tears. Tasting blood, his tongue (which had been slit in several places by rough cardboard) found gaps where teeth had once been. He'd always taken such good care of his teeth too...

Raising his head was a Herculean task, it felt like it was full of pulsing lead. When he finally managed, his body quivered in protest.

One eye was useless, swollen shut. The other was blurry. Blinking was terribly painful. Both his lips were swollen and ruptured. His jaw was probably dislocated. He'd pissed himself at some point, probably sometime between the rubber mallet crushing his testicles against the concrete floor and the car battery cables clamping against the jelly filled sack where they'd once been. Fuck, maybe it was blood instead of piss. He tried to look down, but it hurt too much. Besides, his wrists and ankles were zip tied together.

A lone yellow light hummed and flickered above the sterile room which slowly came back into watery focus. Only then did he notice the blinking red dot above several artificial eyes staring down at him.

Jesus Christ, cameras? They were filming this shit?

Suddenly, it all rushed back to him. The blue-eyed woman and the vice grips. Was this the same room? It sure as Hell looked like it. Holy shit, HOLY SHIT!

His bladder loosed, but his mangled cock couldn't even let it out properly. It dribbled through a half dozen holes drilled by the man with the gas mask. David sobbed.

Just then, a heavy door clanked open and gasmask man waltzed in. Opera music played in the background.

"Glad you're awake, friend. Your bidding has closed. Some degenerate wants to see how long you can last." His voice was all gravel, an Eastern European accent, maybe Russian. "Your government appreciates your service. Dumb cunts like you keep us in business."

"Plwaeth, plwaeth! Mo, dbont."

His voice was more broken than his body.

Gasmask chuckled before sloshing kerosine into his face and over his body. It burned like acid.

"Skazhite d'yavolu, chtoby on prines voskhishcheniye, potomu chto Bog mertv." He snarled, flicking an old-school refillable lighter to life.

Lighting a cigarette, the end glowed orange, just like the camera light on his the laptop he'd burned, and he pulled away the mask long enough to take a deep drag. Then, he tossed the lighter on top of David.

Yellow flame erupted before it even landed with hues of blue at the edges. Writhing and screaming, David felt his body give out from exhaustion and physical destruction, even as his mind screamed.

In the clarity of death, David understood the trap. The whole thing had been a clever set-up to catch dissenters in the act. The illusion of freedom was a chained tiger and his decision to indulge in curiosity had set it free. In death, as in life, he was just another cog in the machine of government.

Bert Lestrange's works include various degrees of Horror, Fantasy, Weird Fiction, and, occasionally, unadulterated Smut. He is the husband of Marie Lestrange, a world traveler and a self-proclaimed foodie—though he has a weakness for gas station chili dogs. He and his family's roots spiderweb across the mountains of East Tennessee. Caregiver, father, and proud ally. Nicest asshole you'll ever meet. Find more of his writing on Godless.com, and two forthcoming novels, STOMPING GROUNDS and an untitled Vampire romance.

Chapter 10

Quantum Marketplace

Marie Lestrange

[FML_Forum]

User: BrokenSoul_35

Posted: January 11, 2025, 6:03 PM EST

Subject: Seeking Solace

Two years. Two fucking years since I lost everything. The silence in this apartment is deafening. I can't stand looking at their photos anymore, but I can't bring myself to take them down either.

I've tried everything– therapy, support groups, even those bullshit online grief forums on the clearnet. Nothing helps and the pain just gets worse. I'm drown-in in cheap whiskey and painful memories, ya'll.

I'm at the end of my rope here. Does anyone know of any... alternative methods? Something on the fringes?

Idc if it's legal or not. I just need to make it stop. Please. I can't do this anymore.

Reply if you have any leads. I'm willing to try anything at this point.

- Jonas

[FML_Forum]

User: QuantumEcho_nlm

Posted: January 11, 2025, 6:17 PM EST

Re: >>>Seeking Solace<<<

@BrokenSoul_35 I feel your pain, brother. I've been where you are. There might be something that could help, but it's not for the faint of heart. Ever heard of the Quantum Marketplace? @QM_Forum is a good place to start, bro. It's deep in the dark web, way beyond the usual drugs and shit. Past the red rooms (which...I don't fucking recommend btw.) They deal in... possibilities. Quantum entangled particles linked to pivotal moments in people's lives.

If you're serious about "alternative methods," this might be what you're looking for. Take it from me, bro, content warning...experience warning...ALL THE WARNINGS. I've heard that reality can get... unstable. It worked out well for me, but it doesn't for everyone. DM me if you want more info. Stay strong, man.

[QM_Forum]

User: BrokenSoul_35

Posted: January 11, 2025, 8:42 PM EST

Subject: Quantum Marketplace - Is this for real?

I've been digging through some seriously weird corners of the dark web for hours now. Keep seeing whispers about this "Quantum Marketplace." At first, I thought it was just another scam, but... I don't know anymore. Some of these posts are talking about altering reality and getting second chances. It sounds insane, but I can't stop reading.

@QuantumEcho_nlm, you mentioned this in your earlier reply. Can you tell me more? Is there any truth to these claims? I know I shouldn't get my hopes up, but... I'm desperate here.

[QM_Forum]

User: QuantumEcho_nlm

Posted: January 11, 2025, 9:10 PM EST

Re: >>>Quantum Marketplace - Is this for real?<<<

@BrokenSoul_35 You're treading into dangerous territory, my friend. The Quantum Marketplace isn't like your typical darknet markets. It deals in something far more valuable and risky than drugs or counterfeit goods. We're talking about quantum-entangled particles linked to pivotal moments in people's lives.

I can guide you there, but you need to understand the risks. This isn't just about avoiding law enforcement. Messing with quantum reality can have unforeseen and irreversible consequences. Reality itself is impacted…it's sum serious shit. Are you sure you want to go down this rabbit hole?

If you're certain, I'll send you a dm with instructions. But remember, once you see behind this curtain, there's no going back.

[QM_Forum]

User: BrokenSoul_35

Posted: January 11, 2025, 9:17 PM EST

Re: >>>Quantum Marketplace - Is this for real?<<<

@QuantumEcho_nlm I appreciate the warning, but I've got nothing left to lose. My reality is already a living hell. If there's even a chance I can change things, I have to try. Please, send me those instructions. I'll do whatever it takes.

[QM_Forum]

User: QuantumEcho_nlm

Posted: January 11, 2025, 9:31 PM EST

Re: >>>Quantum Marketplace - Is this for real?<<<

@BrokenSoul_35 I understand. Check your private messages. I've sent you a series of encrypted links and instructions. Follow them carefully. You'll need to jump through some hoops to prove you're not law enforcement or a bot.

Once you're in, look for the username "Schrodinger's_Merchant." They're your best bet for what you're seeking. Just be careful, my friend. The universe has a way of balancing its books.

Good luck, and may the quantum quell your troubles.

[QM_Forum]

User: BrokenSoul_35

Posted: January 25, 2025, 3:03 AM EST

Subject: I'm in. Holy shit, I'm actually in.

Fuuuuuck Yes! It's been weeks of following breadcrumbs, decrypting messages, and jumping through hoops, but I finally made it!!!!!! The Quantum Marketplace. It's real, and it's more incredible than I could have imagined.

They sent me this weird USB drive thing. Had to give it a blood sample. Felt like something out of a sci-fi movie. But when I plugged it in and logged back into the marketplace... guys, it started listing quantum particles linked to moments in my life. Big moments. Including... the one right before the crash.

Ya'll, I didn't even hesitate. Emptied my savings account. There's apparently some scientist on the other end who can manipulate these particles. Obvs I don't understand any of this quantum shit, but if it'll give me my wife and my kid back....sign me the fuck UP. They said I'd wake up tomorrow and my family would be BACK.

Like a reboot.

I'm terrified and excited and... Idk. As I clicked that "confirm transaction" button, I swear I felt a chill or excitement or adrenaline...some cool universe at work shit, though.

Has anyone else gone through with this? What should I expect? God, I hope this works. I need this to work.

[QM_Forum]

User: QuantumEcho_nlm

Posted: January 25, 2025, 3:31 AM EST

Re: >>>I'm in. Holy shit, I'm actually in.<<<

@BrokenSoul_35 You've taken the plunge. There's no going back now. Results vary. Some wake up to their wildest dreams, others to their worst nightmares. The universe has its way.

Remember what I mentioned before, changing one particle can have unforeseen consequences. "Butterfly" effect and all that. Your family might be back, but at what cost? Be prepared for anything when you wake up. Wouldn't want you to have some Monkey's Paw shit on your hands.

And whatever you do, ***don't try to make any more changes for a while***. Let reality stabilize. Too many alterations too quickly can... fracture things. Badly.

Good luck, man. May the quantum quell your troubles.

[QM_Forum]

User: Schrodingers_Merchant

Posted: January 25, 2025, 4:02 AM EST

Re: >>>>I'm in. Holy shit, I'm actually in.<<<<

Congratulations on your first quantum transaction, @BrokenSoul_35. As the facilitator of your particle manipulation, I must echo @QuantumEcho_nlm's warnings. The entanglement process is delicate, and the outcomes can be unpredictable.

Your chosen particle has been successfully altered. The changes should propagate through your timeline as you sleep. When you wake, your reality may be significantly different. Be prepared for disorientation and possibly conflicting memories.

Remember, the universe seeks equilibrium. What you've gained may come at an unexpected cost. Observe your new reality with care before taking any drastic actions.

If you experience severe reality destabilization (multiple conflicting memories, temporal shifts, etc .), contact me immediately. **Do not** attempt further transactions without consultation.

Sleep well. Your new life awaits. May the Quantum Quell Your Troubles, fine sir!

[QM_Forum]

User: BrokenSoul_35

Posted: February 27, 2025, 7:23 AM EST

Subject: Uhhhhh. Wtf.

I woke up this morning, and...Idk. Ya'll I don't mean to look a gift horse in the mouth but fuck. Everything's changed. My family... they're alive....ish? But nothing is like I thought it would be.

My wife and son are here, but we're miserable. We can't stand each other. There's so much resentment and bitterness. And my parents... they died in the crash instead. I'm parentless, orphaned...*still surrounded by fucking death* in this timeline.

I have two sets of memories competing in my head. I remember the life where I lost them, but I also remember growing up without my parents. It's like my mind is being torn apart in some horcrux voldemort shit or something.

Not a fucking fan.

I thought I was fixing everything, but I've just created a different kind of hell. The guilt is overwhelming. I saved them, and don't get me wrong I am thrilled to have them alive and safe...but fuck. It's like they aren't who they were...and I'm not who I was. It's just...different.

Has anyone else experienced this? How do you cope with the changes? How do I fix this? Them? ME?

[QM_Forum]

User: QuantumEcho_nlm

Posted: February 28, 2025, 3:15am EST

Re: >>>What have I done?<<<

@BrokenSoul_35 Ahhhh, mate. I was wondering when we would hear from you again. Checked the boards every day since hoping we'd get a good report. This is exactly what I was afraid of. The universe always finds a way to balance the scales. You saved your family, but lost your parents and your happiness. It's a cruel trade-off.

The conflicting memories are a common side effect of quantum manipulation. Your mind is trying to reconcile two different timelines. It's disorienting (I know), but it should stabilize over time.

Whatever you do, *don't attempt another transaction right away*. Your reality is already fragile. Give it time to settle before you even think about making any more changes.

Remember, you can't go back to your old timeline. **This** is your reality now. You'll have to find a way to live with the consequences of your choice. Try rebuilding and repairing whatever fractured relationship you have with your family. May the quantum quell you troubles...in time.

@schrodingers_merchant our boy is back...advice?

[QM_Forum]

User: Schrodingers_Merchant

Posted: March 1, 2025, 8:12 AM EST

Re: >>>>What have I done?<<<<

@BrokenSoul_35 Your experience aligns with our observations of quantum entanglement effects on macroscopic scales. The entanglement between particles can lead to unexpected correlations across seemingly unrelated events.

The conflicting memories you're experiencing are a manifestation of quantum superposition at a cognitive level. Your consciousness is essentially entangled across two timelines.

As difficult as it may be, try to view this as an opportunity to study the nature of quantum reality firsthand. Your unique position allows you to observe how changes in quantum states can propagate through complex systems like human relationships and societal structures.

We strongly advise against further manipulations at this time. Allow your quantum state to decohere naturally. Attempting to force changes could lead to severe reality destabilization.

May the Quantum Quell Your Troubles.

[QM_Forum]

User: BrokenSoul_35

Posted: March 11, 2025, 6:00 PM EST

Subject: I can't keep doing this...

I thought I could fix my mistake, but all I've done is make things worse. I tried to undo the changes, thinking maybe I could reset everything back to how it was. But now I'm experiencing *rapid* shifts between timelines...I think?

In one moment, I'm a wealthy businessman with no personal connections—just an empty shell of a man. Then suddenly, I'm a renowned physicist scoot scootin' along in a wheelchair. It's like I'm being pulled apart at the seams. Each shift leaves me more disoriented and panicked.

I_can't_take_it_anymore.

The headaches are unbearable, and I've started getting nosebleeds. It's like my body is trying to tell me that my mind can't handle all this shit.

I've been researching. "Reality Decay"

What the fuck is that supposed to even mean? Is my reality DYING?

I thought I could control this, but it feels like I'm losing grip on everything. Has anyone else experienced these kinds of shifts? How do you deal with the pain and confusion? Obvs I can't go to a doctor over this shit, so strangers on the dark web are my only hope, it seems.

Help a dumbass.

Signed,

Quell My Ass.

P.S. The Quantum could have at least used lube before it FUCKED ME.

[QM_Forum]

User: QuantumEcho_nlm

Posted: April 2, 2025, 6:15 PM EST

Re: >>>I can't keep doing this...<<<

@BrokenSoul_35 This is exactly what happens when you try to manipulate quantum realities without understanding the consequences. The more you attempt to change your timeline, the more fractured your reality becomes. WE TOLD YOU THIS. I know that's not what you wanted to hear, but dammit BrokenSoul! Why didn't you listen to us?

The physical symptoms you're experiencing—headaches and nosebleeds—are manifestations of the strain on your consciousness as it tries to reconcile conflicting memories and experiences. *Your mind is overloaded with information from multiple timelines.*

You need to **stop trying to fix things** immediately. Give yourself time to stabilize in one reality before attempting any further changes. I'll say it again, with the hope that you listen this time...the universe has its own way of balancing things out, and pushing against it will only lead to more chaos.

Take a step back and focus on grounding yourself in your current timeline. You need clarity before you can think about what to do next.

LET THE QUANTUM QUELL YOUR TROU-
BLES and stop fighting it, friend.

[QM_Forum]

User: Schrodingers_Merchant

Posted: April 4, 2025, 6:30 PM EST

Re: <<<<I can't keep doing this...>>>>

@BrokenSoul_35 The phenomenon you're experiencing is known as "reality decay." It occurs when ex-
cessive alterations are made to quantum states without
allowing for proper decoherence. Your consciousness is
caught in a loop of superposition, unable to settle into
a single narrative.

At this point, you must prioritize your mental
health. **Seek out grounding techniques**—medita-
tion, mindfulness, or even just taking a break from
the marketplace altogether may help stabilize your
thoughts.

If you continue to experience severe disorientation or physical symptoms, do not consider reaching out for professional help outside of the quantum realm. You cannot navigate this alone; the stakes are too high, but you cannot make this a publicly acknowledged issue.

Remember, every action has consequences. Allow yourself time to heal before you attempt any further transactions or alterations.

Like Echo said...try and let the quantum quell your troubles. Patience is key.

[QM_Forum]

User: BrokenSoul_35

Posted: May 5, 2025, 1:15 PM EST

Subject: Meeting 'The Creator' - Things are getting serious

So... things are escalating fast. After weeks of digging deeper into the dark web, I finally made contact with a hacker collective led by someone called 'The Creator.' They claim to have inside knowledge about the origins of the Quantum Marketplace who can help me with this "splitting" I keep doing.

We're set to meet in person, but there's a catch. The Creator warned us about some dangerous shit—apparently, there are people out there who want to keep the Marketplace's existence a secret.

Elena and I have been feeling like we're being watched. Yes, I cracked and told her the truth, my wife, love of my life and reason this quantum bullshit is worth it. Unbelievably...that seems to have healed our relationship. Quelled by the quantum or some shit, I guess. Guess I should have trusted it earlier on after all. Lol.

She appreciated that I went to such lengths to bring her back. Anyways, we've noticed shadowy figures following us since we started this journey. It's unsettling and makes me question whether we're in over our heads. Ok, who am I fucking kidding, I was in over my head before I even started!

Has anyone else dealt with this kind of situation? What should we expect from this meeting? I can't shake the feeling that we're stepping into something else there's no turning back from.

[QM_Forum]

User: QuantumEcho_nlm

Posted: May 5, 2025, 6:34 PM EST

Re: <<<Meeting 'The Creator' - Things are getting serious>>>>

@BrokenSoul_35 Meeting with The Creator is a big deal. They hold valuable information that could change everything you know about the Quantum Marketplace. But be cautious—this world is filled with dangers, and not everyone has your best interests at heart.

The shadowy figures could be anyone from rival hackers to government agents trying to shut down the Marketplace. Trust your instincts and stay alert during your meeting.

Make sure you have a secure way to communicate and always have an exit strategy. If things feel off, don't hesitate to walk away. Your safety is paramount.

Keep us updated on what happens. Good luck!

Tagging @schrodingers_merchant so they can weigh in.

[QM_Forum]

User: Schrodinger's_Merchant

Posted: May 5, 2025, 6:37 PM EST

Re: >>>>Meeting 'The Creator' - Things are getting serious<<<<

@BrokenSoul_35 This meeting could provide critical insights into the underlying mechanics of the Quantum Marketplace and its implications for reality manipulation. However, remember that knowledge comes with risks. If The Creator is indeed aware of forces trying to suppress the Marketplace, it may indicate that you're entering a conflict that extends beyond mere transactions. Prepare yourself mentally for what you might learn.

Stay vigilant during your meeting. If you sense danger or feel compromised at any point, prioritize your safety above all else. The world of quantum manipulation is fraught with peril—both from external threats and the unpredictable nature of reality itself. We must protect this particle preference science at great costs.

Stay safe, and may your journey yield the answers you seek.

[QM_Forum]

User: BrokenSoul_35

Posted: May 13, 2025, 1:03 AM EST

Subject: No Subject

Guys, it's not what we thought...

[QM_Forum]

User: QuantumEcho_nlm

Posted: May 13, 2025, 4:32 PM EST

Re: >>>No Subject<<<

@BrokenSoul_35 Dude wtf? You can't just leave us hanging like that. Keep us posted on what happens next. Your safety is paramount, but I also feel like you need to let us in on whatever the hell this means?

@Schrodingers_Merchant SOS

[QM_Forum]

User: Schrodingers_Merchant

Posted: May 13, 2025, 5:07 PM EST

Re: >>>>No Subject<<<<

@BrokenSoul_35 The events you were describing indicate that you are now entangled in a conflict that transcends personal stakes. The Quantum Marketplace has implications far beyond individual transactions—it threatens the very fabric of reality.

The quantum encryption key is a powerful tool but must be handled with extreme caution, and respected, neither of which you did. You did not follow the advice given to you. Now, you will learn actually to accept the consequences of your actions. No do-overs. No quelling. No more.

This is a critical moment; your actions with the Creator determined not just your fate but the fate of many others caught in this web of quantum manipulation.

We'll be in touch...and rest assured that we **will** find you.

The Quantum Comes for You

[QM_Forum]

User: QuantumEcho_nlm

Posted: May 13, 2025, 5:08 PM EST

Stay vigilant and keep us updated on your findings. Your safety is paramount.

[QM_Forum]

User: QuantumEcho_nlm

Posted: May 13, 2025, 5:09 PM EST

Wait. What the fuck @Schrodingers_merchant?!?

[QM_Forum]

User: QuantumEcho_nlm

Posted: May 16, 2025, 5:09 PM EST

Guys wtf is going on!? Are you ok, @Broken_Soul35? Are you there?

@Schrodingers_merchant that sounded threatening, like you're working against our boy, here. What the fuck is happening?

[QM_Forum]

User: QuantumEcho_nlm

Posted: January 12, 2026, 11:12 PM EST

Anything? Just wanting to know that you're ok, @BrokenSoul_35. Send me a DM or somethin man. Hope you're alright.

[QM_Forum]

User: [Deleted]

□User: [Schrodingers_merchant]

▢▢[Fwd:Red Room Forums]

▢▢Tag: NSFW, SNUFF, WARNING

Posted: January 14, 2026, 11:11 PM EST

<u>quantumcode.obscura.room/termina;/cipher/red-room-JonasPunishment/biddingopen/x13/red=room.onion</u>

Marie Lestrange is a multipassionate badass that plays eight musical instruments and is deathly afraid of chickens. She's the author of gothic historical novels Crimson Cobblestones and The Devil's Colony. She hosts a weekly indie Horror podcast called Moths to the Flame. She's obsessed with research into the macabre, true crime, and occultish practices and is also the founding chairman of the Horror Writers Association Tennessee Chapter. When not writing, she and her writer husband, Bert, love traveling with their little Hobbit outside of the East Tennessee mountains they call home.
https://linktr.ee/lestrangebooks

Want More?

Follow along on our social medias
@sinistersociety666
@sinsoc666
www.crimsoncultbooks.com
&
Join our Facebook Group for submissions calls and latest updates!

www.ingramcontent.com/pod-product-compliance
Lightning Source LLC
Chambersburg PA
CBHW020125310726
48970CB00006B/1723